The Castaway

ALSO BY
PIERO RIVOLTA

NOVELS

Alex and the Color of the Wind
Sunset in Sarasota

POETRY

Nothing Is Without Future
Just One Scent

The Castaway

PIERO RIVOLTA

New Chapter
Publisher

Sarasota 2010

Published by New Chapter Publisher

ISBN 978-0-9841745-2-2

New Chapter Publisher
1765 Ringling Blvd.
Suite 300
Sarasota, FL 34236
tel. 941-954-4690
www.newchapterpublisher.com

The Castaway is distributed by Midpoint Trade Books

Printed in the United States of America

Cover design and layout by Shaw Creative
www.shawcreativegroup.com

10 9 8 7 6 5 4 3 2 1

TO MY SON RENZO

You never know which path
will bring you to serenity,
which is by nature temporary
but, like the flowers of the bougainvillea,
keeps re-emerging
covering the thorns.

PART I

JOE THE YANKEE

The Castaway

It was a fine day.

The tropical sun highlighted the different green tones of the lush foliage in the garden that surrounded a simple, one-story, U-shaped building. The main body was fairly long, and the two wings at either end stretched out for about 50 feet. It was a whitish structure dotted with windows of modest dimensions, all closely spaced. The roof was made of galvanized metal. A prefabricated cement wall edged the perimeter of the garden, and on the inside, cutting through the dense, abundant flora, were narrow walkways and open areas marked off with chairs and benches.

He was sitting on one of the benches, looking like a stranger trying to figure out what he was doing there, and wondering what the building and its garden were used for.

He observed his surroundings in intense silence.

His gaze penetrated the scene, but soon his eyes lost all luster, fatigued by the abundant shades of green contrasting with the white of the building and the stretches of grayish cement visible through the thick vegetation.

He sat, listless and self-contained, staring vacantly ahead.

He was beset by a certain inexplicable anxiety that seemed to keep admonishing him. "Don't think, let yourself live." It was like a memory from another life—remnants of experiences much different from his present state and surroundings.

He rose slowly and headed toward the building. There was a door at the center which opened and revealed a tall, lean man with white hair who wore a comfortable open-collared white shirt and dark pants. He looked to be close to 70 and had handsome features, an amicable face that inspired trust. His expression indicated lively intelligence and a resolute manner. He approached the dazed-looking fellow with a smile, took him by the arm, and guided him inside the building.

The interior was quite simple.

It looked like the waiting room in an old clinic or a school: clean, bare, with chairs lined up along the wall and a small table with a telephone in a corner. The floor was covered with light-colored tiles; the walls were a faded but soothing shade of green. The ceiling was white and steepled, following the triangular shape of the rafters.

After the almost physical force of the vivid sun outside, the pleasant, dim interior offered a sense of protection.

The man with the white hair took a chair and placed it facing another. He invited his companion to sit and took his hands into his own. He looked at him intensely and began speaking in a mild voice.

"Are you bored here? You appear distracted, not paying attention to yourself and what's around you. It's as if you were not aware of other people's existence.

You speak to no one.

But you can talk to me—you speak my language. Judging from the few words you've spoken since you arrived, I'd say you come from a place not very far from the part of the world where I grew up. I was born in New Jersey, close to New York."

He paused, hoping the other would reply or at least nod.

But there was no sign. Only silence.

The older man went on, "I've had a somewhat nomadic life myself, sometimes even adventurous.

I spent my youth in New Jersey. After college I got a job in the headquarters of a large distribution company and was fairly successfully climbing the corporate ladder. But one day I felt an irresistible urge, a calling that beckoned me to help others and to explain to them that the essence of life is love. I was not driven by a purely religious motive. Actually, with my free spirit, I could not stomach all those 'petty' rules that every religion seeks to impose.

One day I met an extraordinary man, a great thinker, with whom I began discussing the general problems of life. I ended up opening my soul to him. I revealed my doubts: the little mysteries and secrets that each one of us has. He was a Jesuit.

His arguments were certainly not those of an ordinary Catholic priest, and clearly very different from the flock of televangelists whom I considered vaudeville actors not worth my time or attention. My opinion of them hasn't changed."

He stopped for a second; then, holding the other man's eyes, he continued. "To put it briefly, after many years of study I became a Jesuit myself, and I traveled the world with the aim of explaining that it is not the religious rules created by men that are important, but only the love that is part of all of us. For us Jesuits it comes from Jesus, while for others it comes from the sun or a universal force, and some other spiritual belief and divinity. The only thing that counts is love and the continuous search for it, whether through philosophy, art, poetry, sacrifice, faith or grace.

Do you understand what I'm trying to tell you?"

The man raised his eyes to the ceiling. He seemed to be waking as if from a deep sleep and muttered only, "I understand very well what you have said, but I do not know how to reply."

The Jesuit took a deep breath. At last he had succeeded in making a tiny opening. He recalled the words of wisdom that had guided him through his studies: I must be patient and persistent. But as he rose from his chair, all he said was, "Let's go eat. The others have already gone to the dining hall."

The Castaway

2

The dining hall was crowded, yet hushed. Most of the ten rectangular tables seated between six and eight people. Several female servers brought food and drink—mainly water—in an uninterrupted flow. The man noted the subdued chatter among the clanging of plates and flatware, and a few smiles passing among some of the tablemates.

Nearly everyone in the room was dressed in white—white shirts with collars and T-shirts. Only a few bright colors here and there broke up the monotony. The entire meal took place in a general atmosphere of tranquil satisfaction.

The man ate with pleasure. For the first time in weeks he felt interested in observing others and yielding to the stimulus to ask himself questions about the people around him. He observed his tablemates with newfound curiosity.

They were all focused on "the job" of eating, intent on fulfilling the primary human necessity—nourishment. It seemed to him that they practically had raised the daily ritual to the level of art, an art born from centuries of research and practice to satisfy the tastes of so many and to make mealtimes a special social occasion.

The Jesuit sat at another table with only three others. He observed the gathering and offered an embracing smile, first to one table, then to the next. Watching him with interest, our man thought that the priest was trying to send them a message, though perhaps it was just his imagination.

"Who knows why these people live here?" the man asked himself. "Do they know my name and where I come from? I wonder why I am here.

The Jesuit told me he didn't know. Was he being sincere, or was he just looking for an excuse to get me to talk?

And what about him? Who is this unusual priest? What's he doing here? What's his role?

Everyone addresses him with the respect due a leader, yet he behaves with modesty and ease. He takes in everyone and everything, and he converses effortlessly with guests and the people who run this strange hostel—or is it a clinic?"

In truth, the atmosphere was similar to a sanatorium. During the meal, the servers in white uniforms also distributed medicine according to instructions written on large sheets of paper.

The man's subconscious kept prodding him with questions.

"Am I in a hospital or a nursing home? Come to think of it, this seems like a place for the depressed, or even... the insane.

Maybe I've gone mad!

How ironic, considering how long I spent looking for a place where clocks were useless, where time didn't matter, where Marianne lived waiting for me, and…now I've wound up in a nuthouse, where people don't speak my language; or if they do, they barely manage a few broken words or phrases—except for the Jesuit.

This is surely a place where I don't belong.

I'm haunted by the memory of the turquoise sea, a small catamaran, Marianne's face, the white coast of western Florida speeding off behind us. Then…then…nothing.

And now here I am among these strangers, talking to a Jesuit. Me. The closest I ever got to the Catholic church was seeing the pope on television. The pope. I have to admit, it was somewhat fascinating to see him decked out in his regalia, looking truly inspired among all those bishops and cardinals, and surrounded by the beautiful architecture of St. Peter's Basilica, grand and majestic, in contrast to the smallness of man. And the crowd applauding in ecstasy.

I really need to figure out what I am doing here!"

When lunch was over, he got up and headed to the door. No one spoke to him. A server walked toward him as if to stop him, but the Jesuit shook his head at her. Then he smiled at our man as if to say, "Go ahead. Go think. Go ask yourself those questions whose answers are tied to the meaning of your life. I'll join you and aid you in your search."

The man received the message and absorbed it like a sea sponge longing to fill itself with the ocean water from which it had been torn.

The Castaway

He entered a large, simply furnished room. There were many small, square tables and hard plastic chairs scattered about. Normally the guests gathered there to read, draw, play cards or dominoes, and engage in various other entertainment, but now it was empty.

For the first time, he realized that he was not treated like the others. The attendants left him to spend his time in whatever way he wanted.

After he sat in his chair for some time, a woman with dark, glossy hair approached him. She was not very tall but well built and spoke English mixed with Spanish expressions, some of which were not clear to him. But he understood that the attendant was trying to communicate to him that it would be better if he went to his room to rest like all the others, and that after the siesta, he could participate in the various activities.

He smiled. He always smiled because he wanted to appear polite. In truth, he longed to scream out to everybody to leave him alone, but he did not wish to embarrass the woman.

He got up, saying "muchas gracias" with his Yankee accent, and followed her toward his room. She looked at him with amazement, but she was satisfied. Never before had she heard him speak.

When he arrived at the small double room, his roommate was already there. He was a kind, elderly man who had refined manners, always smiling at our man and showing much attention to the things he did.

Besides Spanish, this fellow knew a number of words in English, at least enough to communicate essential needs. The two treated one another with respect, but used the excuse of their differing languages to remain isolated, each locked in his own world. Both suspected that, with minimal effort, they could break the ice and communicate with one another in one language or the other, but they had decided to make no attempt in that regard.

Although they shared the same room, they came from separate worlds, and their personal habits influenced their behavior. In addressing one another, they used the names Joe and Manuel, but they did not react automatically to them when called, indicating that both names were the fruit of purest invention.

They had a single aim in common—the defense of their privacy. Only in this were they alike.

Joe had always had the sensation that he was alone. But now he felt it even more intensely because of the false name he had assumed. He had made it up on the spot when someone asked him, "Who are you?"

Lately, he'd been asked this question many times.

One night he was lying in bed trying to go to sleep. The regular breathing of his elderly roommate recalled to his mind the time when he was first asked this question.

He had just regained consciousness in a tiny cabin on an unfamiliar ship. He still remembered the constant buzzing sound accompanied by slight vibrations which, in a certain way, were reassuring.

His body ached all over. He felt a cold sensation, but when he touched himself, his skin felt blistered and roasted. He could barely open one eye. There was a damp cloth on his head.

He was able to make out a figure dressed in white beside him, who was searching for something inside a box lying on a small shelf.

He felt an enormous emptiness in his heart. What was he doing in this place that looked like a ship's cabin? It may have been part of the process of his liberation, but he doubted it.

Because he was aware of his aching body, he suddenly realized that the timeless existence he had been sharing with a wonderful woman might have been just a dream or a lost reality.

Surely, something must have gone wrong.

He groaned and moved ever so slightly. The man next to him was startled and turned to look. He had an open but worried face, and when he spoke his English had a slight South American accent.

"Can you talk?"

Receiving no reply, he continued, "I'm the chief officer on this cargo ship, and I have a little experience in first aid.

Stay calm, everything's all right. You're dehydrated, you've got a very bad sunburn. I've given you an injection and covered you with ointment. I've also given you a painkiller. Luckily, you were able to swallow some liquid.

11

You'll be sent to a hospital shortly.

Lie still. I'm going to put in an IV, and then you'll sleep, you'll see."

The castaway made no reply, just moved his mouth slightly as if to say thank you, although he wasn't sure whether he should thank the man or curse him for having roused him from a lovely dream.

Before leaving the cabin, the chief officer asked him, "Can you tell me who you are and where you come from?"

He shook his head in desperation. He picked the first name that came to mind and stammered, "Joe, I think. But I can't remember my last name."

He heard the other man's voice, as if from far away. "Don't worry about it. Rest."

Once again he abandoned himself to nothingness. His head began to spin, his mouth was dry and his mind exhausted.

One word, however, he sighed through his parted lips: Marianne.

The Castaway

4

That afternoon the Jesuit, who everyone called "Padre Brian," drove to the local police station, as he had done often during the past two months, to report on Joe's convalescence.

Joe had been found in the open sea by a merchant ship traveling from the port of Tampa to Vera Cruz. It usually followed a course further north, but there had been a low-pressure storm system in the center of the Gulf of Mexico which was moving northwest, so the ship took a more southwesterly direction toward the Yucatan Peninsula.

Late one morning, with the sun high in the sky, a crew member spotted what looked like a raft floating in the water. It turned out to be a catamaran in bad shape, with its sails gone. It was being dragged along by the strong Gulf currents.

The routine on a ship can often become monotonous, so the captain welcomed the distraction and decided to approach what he figured was a small abandoned craft that the tides had "abducted" from a beach. All the crew looked on with curiosity as they drew closer, some shading their eyes against the blinding sun with their arms, others using binoculars to get a better view. When it began to dawn on them that there might be a body on the catamaran, their curiosity turned to apprehension.

The ship reduced its speed and approached the battered boat slowly. Letters and numbers were no longer visible on the hull, only the manufacturer's logo. It was one of the most popular models.

The suspicion that there might be someone on board turned out to be valid. The crew watched in uneasy silence as an unconscious man was lifted up the ladder to the freighter. He was a Caucasian, probably from the Florida coast. He was breathing, but in bad shape—dehydrated and sunburned.

There was no real doctor on board, but the chief officer attended to the man and advised the captain to steer the ship closer to the Yucatan coast and call for help, since Vera Cruz was still too far away. The crew, anxious about being stuck with a sick man aboard, heaved a sigh of relief when their ailing passenger was taken off the ship and helicoptered to a Yucatan hospital.

The castaway stayed there for 15 days.

In the meantime, the local authorities started an investigation in search of the man's name and origin. They were hoping to locate an address so he could be repatriated, and to perhaps find someone to pay for the costs incurred during his rescue and hospital stay. Since the castaway spoke English, the U.S. consulate was informed and a functionary was appointed to the case. The U.S. Coast Guard was contacted to find out whether any missing persons report had been filed in connection with the man's catamaran.

There wasn't one, and the mystery persisted. One theory was that the catamaran belonged to a large yacht or cruise ship, whose auxiliary craft had somehow cut loose. But after two weeks, the authorities were no wiser than before.

Meanwhile, the castaway's condition had improved physically, but he appeared distant, as if he had no desire to live.

His mood may have been the consequence of having been so close to death, of having experienced extreme solitude so intensely.

At first he spoke very little, and hesitantly at that. He seemed to want to tell them, "Leave me alone, by now I'm part of another world."

They thought he might be under the influence of a drug, but the blood tests showed no sign of it.

It was impossible to tell how long he had been at sea, but it certainly must have been more than a week. In truth, he was a well-built man who proved to be quite strong by recovering so quickly from his adventure.

To the insistent questions of the police and hospital staff, he responded that he remembered his name was Joe, but nothing more.

He spoke with a clear American accent, typical of the northeastern United States. His way of moving and reacting was similar to that of the tourists from that part of the world as well. So they called him "Joe the Yankee" in honor of old movies about the American Civil War.

Joe thanked everyone for the attention they were giving him, but he repeatedly asked, "Why have you brought me here instead of leaving me on that catamaran out at sea? I was fine there, I was happy." Then he immediately added, so as not to appear ungrateful, "Not that I don't like it here. You have all been so kind. I just wonder whether my presence is of any use other than inconveniencing so many people. I dreamed marvelous tales while at sea…"

For the authorities, the situation represented both a legal and financial dilemma, as well as an immigration problem. They did not know what to do with Joe until a functionary at the U.S. Consulate had the idea of contacting Padre Brian. As a man who had dedicated his life to helping others, he was the head of an organization that provided care for children, the elderly, the disabled, victims of Alzheimer's disease, and people whose mental faculties were impaired.

This organization helped people in part through home-care assistance, in part through residential facilities located in various neighborhoods around town. They took in people who required care for only a few hours a day, as well as more complicated cases for whom the centers functioned as actual nursing homes.

Besides local funding, Padre Brian's organization also benefited from important international donors, and enjoyed the backing of the Jesuit Order.

When the consulate approached him with the request, Padre Brian agreed and promised to take care of Joe the Yankee until his identity was discovered. He would also keep in contact with the local police and the American Consulate.

The authorities were relieved. Since everything about the castaway was such a mystery, no one really knew what to do about him. He was, in short, a "hot potato," and they were glad to leave him in the hands of the good padre.

The Jesuit welcomed the challenge as an occasion to affirm the values of life by attempting to communicate with Joe.

He also relished the opportunity to overcome the complicated bureaucratic disorganization typical of nations when they try to communicate with one another.

When it came down to it, every country faced its share of similar little everyday problems and handled them in more or less the same fashion. Yet when asked to collaborate to find a common solution, they preferred to view them as decidedly American problems, Mexican problems, Chinese problems, German problems, Palestinian problems, Israeli problems, and so on.

Walking back to his car from the police station that first day, Padre Brian had muttered to himself, "Doesn't anyone remember what Jesus Christ tried to teach us? The churches certainly have forgotten. We've once again gone back to the Old Testament – 'An eye for an eye,' and 'Die, Samson! Along with all the Philistines.' Back to the Koran, and holy war against the infidels.

What infidels? Infidels of what religion?

Religion should be a means to seek out love, understanding, sharing and forgiveness – a guide for improving respect and love for others, for oneself, for the world.

What does it matter whether Jesus was truly the son of God, or God himself, or just an exceptional man?

We're all children of God, but Christ put forth the message of love, which is as relevant as ever, and which everyone can follow. Though in reality many believers and churches of all denominations seem to ignore it."

Whenever he got worked up like this, Padre Brian no longer knew whether he was cursing his own religion or playing at being Jesus in the temple.

A shiver ran down his spine. He shook himself and looked about as if to get a bead on the reality surrounding him. He grinned. No one had witnessed his outburst.

No bolt of lightning had struck him down.

This was, then, a new era, in which God was more tolerant. Perhaps the Old Testament really was something that belonged to the past.

The Castaway

5

This afternoon at police headquarters, Padre Brian learned once again that there was no news regarding Joe's identity. On his part, he could assure the authorities that the presumed American was improving and he would soon be able to remember what had happened to him.

When events lose their color of novelty, they are forgotten and fade into the haze of everyday normalcy. So the priest's report was treated with a sense of casual indifference by the authorities who had been urged to find a quick answer to Joe's mystery immediately after the rescue.

They said, "All right, Padre. We have extreme faith in you. You always find a good solution. Thank you all the same for coming by."

It was still early when Padre Brian headed back. Having a few errands to run and a few repair jobs to check up on that afternoon, he decided to go get Joe and take him along. The jaunt might do him good; perhaps it would help him feel closer to the habits of his former life.

He found Joe sitting in the garden, and with the pretext that he needed help, the priest easily convinced him to come along.

The station wagon was old, but comfortable enough, and the air conditioning worked.

As they drove through the town, the Jesuit glanced at his passenger. He had already noted that Joe possessed a highly sensitive, yet generous spirit. He demonstrated an unusual capacity for picking up the nuances of situations in a heartbeat.

"I wonder what his real name is," Padre Brian thought. "He doesn't seem to react naturally to the name Joe. It's as if every time someone calls him, he has to think it through or wake from a dream."

They passed through narrow side streets and small squares, stopping from time to time to buy something, talk to someone, negotiate with a store owner, visit the home of a senior citizen or simply greet the people who spoke to them.

For Joe it was all a pleasant distraction. He was surprised how good it felt to accompany Padre Brian, who was so well known and respected. Everyone responded to him with such politeness and nonchalant good cheer. Joe wondered whether this was due to the normal customs of the people in that area, or whether it was Padre Brian's presence that influenced their behavior.

It didn't take him long to reach the conclusion that the people of this place were cordial by nature – and this gave him enormous gratification. He felt satisfied and his heart began to open.

After each errand, the two returned to the close but comfortable interior of the automobile, sitting next to each other in shared intimacy. As Padre Brian had foreseen, the afternoon's brief excursion helped to improve their relationship, producing a new feeling of complicity and growing ease between them.

Padre Brian's life was by now quite removed from a strictly ecclesiastical existence. He was full of second thoughts and questions about religion, which he put off by keeping busy, consumed with his everyday responsibilities and commitments to others. But he was still a Jesuit, and he carried with him—as if he had been indelibly branded—the keenness of thought, the refined style of reasoning, and the attention to the human spirit that the order developed not only among its members, but also, in part, in the people who attended its educational institutions.

Padre Brian began talking about himself to help Joe feel at ease. The work I do appears to have very little importance, and perhaps that's so, but I feel as gratified doing it as a man can feel."

As he turned onto a wider street, he let a few seconds of silence settle between them before he continued. "You'll have to excuse me. I don't know whether you're a believer or not, and in what religion. I don't want to confuse you, talking about me. You see, I'm a special kind of priest. I don't really conform completely to the Vatican's rules, even if I have profound faith in what awaits us in the afterlife."

He stared at Joe as if to ask, "Should I go on, or would you prefer that I stop?"

For the first time since they'd met, he saw in Joe's eyes a flicker of interest.

Thus encouraged, he continued. "You see, I have had many years of intense study of history and philosophy, and I was taught the practice of examining the same problem from different points of view without ever discarding the opinions of others or of other religions.

This process leaves a profound mark, which each one of us may apply differently deep within ourselves. In any case, it leads us to the assessment of various concepts and the careful consideration of the use of certain words.

I'll give you an example. What do the words eternal and infinite mean?

We use them in poetry, in sermons, in science, even in the most banal pop songs. In mathematics, two parallel lines are defined as two lines that meet only at infinity. Mathematics has even assigned a well-defined symbol to represent the concept of infinity. Is this symbol all we know about it?"

He drove slowly, his eyes glued to the road, as if keeping the car moving ahead was his only goal.

But then he turned and looked at Joe. The new light in Joe's eyes pleased him.

He pointed out a building not far off amid the greenery and said, "Later we'll go there. It's a kindergarten. First we have to go pick up my printer, which I've had overhauled."

He paused briefly before continuing, "If we try to tackle the concept of eternity, we feel lost. We get the shivers just trying to imagine it. Either that, or we abandon the idea, especially nowadays, when we're so used to considering minutes, even thousandths of seconds, as important features of our existence.

But whatever our attitude toward eternity, whether we believe it has the possibility to become a reality, or whether we

refuse it entirely, if we are honest with ourselves, we have to admit that it profoundly intrigues us.

We can't imagine a timeless world, a world that isn't marked by sunrises and sunsets, though deep down inside we want to believe that eternity exists. Worse yet, when we mock it or deny it, we give it substance and make belief in its existence all the more real. The problem is imagining it."

Joe burst into sonorous, pleasant laughter.

When he had recovered, he said, "How glad I am to see that you live in the same confusion as I do...or maybe the same confusion we all live in?"

They say laughter is contagious and indeed, Padre Brian roared too, delighted to have found an inroad to Joe's spirit. And he committed a small sin of pride when he thought, "Once again, reason and the desire to communicate have come to my rescue. I'm not such an inept Jesuit after all."

The Castaway

The station wagon pulled into the schoolyard of the kindergarten. It was recess, and many children milled about, hardly listening to the teachers' orders. They were divided into groups, and each group was busy with its own game.

Just as the car came to a halt, it seemed as if everything stopped. As Padre Brian opened his door and emerged from the vehicle, he was greeted by the children cheerfully shouting as one.

His eyes twinkled.

For the first time, Joe understood why this man, so eclectic and profound, derived so much satisfaction from his work.

The teachers called for a return to order, but the children who had reached the car paid them no mind and crowded around Padre Brian, eager to attract his attention.

Witnessing the scene, Joe felt like a stranger, or rather, like a novice taking his first step into an unknown world.

Some of the more obedient children continued playing without conviction, their attention wandering toward the new arrivals. The rest, along with the teachers, helped Padre Brian unload the station wagon. Joe lifted up a large box and was surprised to realize that he was participating in the activity, and enjoying it.

As they walked toward the building, the entrance to the school opened.

A woman appeared in the doorway. She was wearing a blue skirt and a white short-sleeved blouse with a wide collar that was open in front. She had long legs, a thin waist and well-proportioned hips. Her eyes were green, her hair was very dark and not too long. She looked to be less than 40, though she may have been a few years older. At any rate, she looked quite young.

What struck Joe was the woman's sober elegance, her open face and her bright smile, which blossomed when she saw Padre Brian.

She walked toward the priest, shook his hand and kissed him on the cheek. The Jesuit's eyes lit up. He introduced his passenger, "This is Joe, an American who 'dropped in' on us. You certainly are familiar with these kinds of surprises well enough."

The woman laughed gracefully and replied in perfect English, "Nice to meet you, Joe. Welcome. I hope you like it here. This place is a little different, but it has its intriguing, even enthralling— "

Joe, who had been watching her with growing excitement, interrupted, "I'm finding that out through direct experience. Spending the day with Padre Brian has been an eye-opener, and coming to this kindergarten has cleared up a lot for me."

"You're lucky to get to know one of the most positive experiences in our little world dedicated to helping those in need," she replied. "I hope you won't be disappointed by the rest of us."

Joe suddenly remembered the way he used to relate to attractive women in his previous life. He smiled and said gallantly, "After meeting you, I don't think there's anything left in Mexico to see."

Padre Brian glanced at Joe with an expression that hovered somewhere between curiosity and contentment.

Perhaps his new friend was starting to come around.

Adopting a professional tone, he said, "Joe, this kind woman is Sara. She's the director of this school. She's an American citizen, born in New York—although her father was British and her mother was Mexican. She speaks perfect English and Spanish, and also knows French, Portuguese and Italian.

She's a gift bestowed upon us by Providence, though unfortunately for a limited time only—we don't know how long, but we intend to exploit her talents to the fullest while she's here!"

Sara's eyes danced with mischief. "Don't believe everything Padre Brian says. He is too fond of paying compliments."

Padre Brian protested good-naturedly. "No one's ever said that of me. Actually, if truth be known, I tend to be a bit grumpy, though I do know how to appreciate graciousness in others."

For a moment, the three stood there in silence. Then Sara turned and led them inside.

To Joe it felt as if something important had remained hanging in the air. It reminded him of a television program which ends just as things are beginning to get interesting, but you have to wait for the next episode. "Tune in next week, same time, same channel."

He followed Sara inside like a kindergartner with a bounce in his step.

The change in his attitude didn't go unnoticed by Padre Brian.

The Castaway

7

This Sara is very interesting and very attractive, don't you think?" Padre Brian remarked as the station wagon proceeded down the dirt road.

When Joe didn't react, he continued. "You know, Joe, I haven't always been a Jesuit. Once I had the good fortune to experience true love. But things didn't work out as I'd planned. They say the ways of the Lord are infinite—it's just a saying, but there's a lot of truth to those words."

He paused, letting this sink in.

"Believe me, I've experienced it directly, and I have been witness to many other cases."

Joe didn't respond.

"Don't you believe it?"

The question hung in the air. No reply, no comment. Padre Brian remained silent, sizing Joe up like a painter who, after completing a most masterful brushstroke, steps back from the canvas to get a better view of the effect. Still nothing.

They drove along slowly, passing houses, trees and shrubs. Padre Brian turned on the radio. Mexican folk music was playing. The singers repeated the many refrains with different vocal intonations.

After a few minutes, Joe shifted uncomfortably in his seat and said, "Padre, can you turn off the radio? I like music. It's just that it's bothering me right now. Even if I find the silence oppressive, too."

"Then say something!" Padre Brian exclaimed. "Say whatever comes to mind. Or sing. Or curse. Just so long as you don't take the Lord's name in vain—even if He is very understanding about that sort of thing.

Don't worry about me being here. I often talk to myself, sometimes I really get carried away.

You see, many people believe that a priest is different from them. In part, it may be true. But as far as I'm concerned, I often mix up the various roles I play in life. I confuse what it is to be a man, a priest and a Jesuit.

Of course, the Jesuit always tries to find a compromise between the other two."

When Joe didn't respond to his attempt to lighten the mood, Padre Brian hesitated, but only for a moment. Then he continued with determination.

"We've got one last package to deliver—to the center where you're staying. I've got an idea. Go to your room, get your things and come to my house for dinner. I'll treat you to some good whiskey, the one I save for special occasions. You could spend the night, stay a few days if you like. I've got a comfortable guest room."

Although Joe seemed reluctant, Padre Brian pressed on, "Do say you'll come. It would be a chance for me to relax and take a break, a pleasant detour from the more difficult challenges of my profession.

What do you say?

Will you allow me the pleasure of sharing my table with you?"

The Jesuit fixed Joe with clear, bright eyes. Their calm expression of strength demanded an answer.

Joe turned and stared straight ahead. Then he muttered a terse "Yes," followed by a small nod.

Less than an hour later, Padre Brian opened the front door to his home to let Joe enter.

The Castaway

8

It is said that guests are like fish—after three days they begin to stink. But in Joe's case, days became weeks without any sign of decay in his relationship with his host. People in town got so used to seeing Padre Brian in his station wagon with his American helper alongside him that they stopped making comments about it.

It was during this extended stay that Joe learned Padre Brian's story. After dinner, they would repair to the living room, where over a glass of whiskey or two, the priest would reveal bits and pieces of his former life, along with occasional philosophical excursions and political observations.

Padre Brian was born Brian Christopher, into a middle-class American family in a small town in New Jersey. His mother and father had grown up there, too, not far from one another. Thinking back to life with his family, Padre Brian recalled having moved only once.

It had happened when his father, who worked at the head-quarters of a wholesale distribution company, changed jobs. His new position came with a substantial salary hike. Not long afterward he bought a more comfortable and spacious home. His mother worked part-time as a nurse at the hospital.

For Brian, life proceeded with great regularity, barely touched by the great international upheavals and social changes which appeared on the American horizon following World War II. In real terms, the wars and tensions that gripped the world had no effect on his daily routine, which consisted of work, home, friendships, church, hobbies, sports and an occasional vacation trip to the mountains, the ocean or a national park.

Padre Brian remembered those times as a period when life seemed simpler. Since then, things had gotten busier. The cold winters and the hot summers seemed to leave less and less time for spring and fall. The advent of the space age hurried the world along, just as the flow of automobile traffic ballooned to drastic proportions.

As someone who was curious about history, Brian knew, however, that while technology changed quickly, when it came down to it, the essential daily routines didn't change all that much for most people.

The great social engine that is the U.S.A. continued to churn out ideas, overcome crises, re-invent itself to offer its citizens work and security.

In the process, everyone exercised the right and the privilege to dream and make their dreams come true, big or small, material or spiritual. Except for occasional jolts, everything functioned like a smoothly running machine. The socio-political system laid down by the Founding Fathers adapted itself to new conditions. Progress and growth continued unabated.

Growth. What did the word mean? No one really ever understood it. It was supposed to be the future.

Heady thoughts for a teenager, yet…for the moment, days passed and people were happy to achieve small goals—a new home, new furniture, a new car, a bigger TV, more credit at the bank.

Small but important conquests when it came to living and trying to answer the eternal question, "What is the meaning of our lives?"

That is the recurring question, forever surfacing from the bottom of our souls, one which we don't like to ask ourselves very often—otherwise it might take away our desire to breathe.

Joe was startled to learn that Padre Brian had struggled with the same question that gnawed at him.

Brian attended the local schools and did very well. But what surprised him and his family was how much he loved the outdoors, especially the mountains. He came to feel that he had lived for too long in the low hills of New Jersey, with its long sandy beaches.

During vacations he'd traveled to the west coast of the United States, where the natural beauty and powerful—at times even bizarre—landscapes fascinated him. How fond he was of wandering among the mountains, canyons, lakes, streams, and, in the late afternoon, watching the northern California sun sink into the ocean.

The panoramas of tiny beaches set against imposing rocky spurs and outcroppings took his breath away.

He found the churning ocean to be a mystery and a wonder, never still and populated by such an amazing quantity of life forms. But Brian came to realize that he was more attracted by those majestic cliffs that descended straight into the water.

He became convinced that his true passion was the mountains, the real ones, made of rock and stone, poised over aspen and pine forests as if to stand watch over the valleys, lakes and rivers. He felt protected and, at the same time, intimidated by their imposing presence.

It's true: even though man seeks freedom, he is unconsciously attracted by everything that looms above him and dominates him—whether it be tall mountains, church steeples, skyscrapers, religion, ideas and passions of all sorts—which actually circumscribe man's freedom to act.

Brian did not, however, experience this sensation of being confined in Colorado, where, once you mounted one ridge, another immediately appeared before you. Hiking there, everything seemed to continue on, infinitely.

What a pretty illusion!

At the time, though, Brian was happy whenever he visited the Rockies. It was the only time when he felt whole.

Before finishing high school, he made up his mind that he would attend the University of Colorado at Boulder. The school wasn't inexpensive for non-Colorado residents, and it was pretty tough to get in. But with the promise of financial support from his father, who would have preferred to see him at a college on the east coast closer to home, he worked hard and was accepted.

For Brian it was a huge change in lifestyle. The routine that had accompanied him for many years became, in a few short seconds, ancient history. The complex organism that was the university and the stimulus provided by the crisp, clear mountain air filled him with energy he had never felt before.

At school, his days were populated by many new acquaintances. The experiences derived from these relationships, both with his professors and schoolmates, aroused in Brian a new awareness of communication. He soon understood that university life was a closed system with its own rules and people who knew how to manipulate the game.

He discovered, to his great surprise, that he had a natural flair for playing this game, and each day brought him growing respect and admiration from the community where he lived.

His four years in Boulder were intense years, full of contradictions, emotions and, at times, confusion—the stuff that makes people grow spiritually.

He got involved in many campus experiences—the good ones, the less than good ones, and even those that were officially outlawed—but his participation was always somewhat detached. In that way, he was typical of those who dabbled at all kinds of things in order to judge them firsthand and be able to say they knew what they were all about without ever having to commit themselves.

With this approach he developed a reputation as a person of solid character, someone people could count on, even if his behavior occasionally seemed awkward and aloof. In addition, his manner, which often came off as stiff, seemed to contrast with his open views, which were always directed toward the future.

In reality, he was ready to revise his opinions if new developments were convincing enough.

Many turned to him for advice and for help, or engaged him to negotiate with professors in order to smooth out the inevitable differences between students and the teaching staff. Practically speaking, he assumed, without endeavoring to do so, the role of a wise Indian chief who tries to satisfy his people while bargaining with the white man.

He developed two male friendships. His comrades were quite different from him, but they all shared a love for the outdoors. They got along well together without a great deal of soul searching, whether it was on campus or in the mountains, where they sought respite and refuge from the "game" whenever they could.

His relationships with the opposite sex, however, were more complicated. He liked girls and spent a lot of time with them.

Girls think differently from guys, and this intrigued him very much. At parties he often preferred hanging out with groups of girls, because he found their conversation more stimulating. He liked how they enriched his experience and helped him improve his communication skills.

In this way, he developed close relationships with many members of the opposite sex, acting as a confidante for their many secrets. That position, however, inevitably precluded any romantic involvement. Once he became a trusted friend, he had to give up any possibility of sexual involvement.

in the beginning, playing confidante made him feel special and gratified, especially when he compared himself to his male peers. But soon there grew within him the feeling that he was being excluded from the lively game of courtship. The worst part was that many times he would hear from both the girl and her current lover the story of their respective feelings. On top of this, he would often be asked to keep everything secret, and conduct a series of interventions to help the lovebirds overcome difficult moments.

But who was Brian? A priest people confessed to? A psychologist, a clever go-between? More and more he truly felt like that Indian chief, upon whom the whole tribe depended for his wisdom.

While the others were using him as an astute and neutral mediator, he was struggling with his identity and frustrated by his isolation and inability to connect on a physical level.

At his lowest moments, he questioned whether he would ever be able to love and be loved.

Meanwhile, he continued his studies with success. Following in his father's footsteps, he majored in business administration. He expected to complete his Bachelor's degree with honors, after which he would decide whether it was worth getting a Master's in Boulder or at some other university, or go back to New Jersey to find a job.

He was fairly certain that, given his father's reputation and his grades, he could find a promising position. The course of his future was clearly mapped out.

At the beginning of his senior year, however, something unexpected happened. In what was by now a large circle of familiar friends whose demands required considerable investment of time and energy on his part, a pretty new female student made her appearance.

Her name was Anne. She was slightly more than a year younger than him, and had transferred from another university.

Perhaps as a newcomer she felt a bit uncomfortable at first. Maybe it was because, like him, she loved to get away to the mountains; or because she was a very contemplative person (she often came out with simple but keen observations). Perhaps it was the combination of these characteristics. In any case, Anne saw in Brian her Prince Charming.

As for Brian, he was surprised by a new feeling inside himself, a reaction she seemed to create in him.

Thanks to his encounters with Anne, Brian had the opportunity to find out the answers to the questions that had haunted him, and to experience what being in love means.

The Castaway

9

Conversations between Padre Brian and Joe were lively and varied. Topics ranged from everyday problems to customs and habits in the Yucatan, from the various people they met during the day's routine to Mexican and international politics.

Joe came to be acquainted with the way people related to one another in this part of Mexico, which was much different, for example, from the central part of the country around Mexico City.

Here lived a genuine, hard-working people. They perhaps got a bit carried away with their Catholicism, but it was also their strength, the glue that made them a homogeneous population. It also seemed to Joe that they practiced their religion with much seriousness and a great sense of practicality—an example for other religious communities to follow.

The religious system was a help that made up for the absence of the state, and was accepted without fanaticism.

They were interesting discussions, considering that both Joe and Padre Brian shared a common background. Both had been born and had lived in the United States—a nation so open, yet at the same time so intense that it left an indelible mark on people. Though they may not wish to admit it, deep down in their hearts they would always remain Americans.

Indeed, Padre Brian, despite his wealth of adventures far from home, would always be a Jesuit, and what's more, an American Jesuit.

As Joe learned more of Padre Brian's "private" stories and identified with the Jesuit's tales, he resolved to open himself up a bit, and even shared a few of his own experiences.

Thus, his host learned that Joe had been married to a woman named Marianne, who was the love of his life. They'd met while working in the financial sector on Wall Street. Having become disenchanted with the superficial nature of their New York existence, they decided to change their lifestyle and move to Florida.

But while Brian's stories were full of details and emotions, Joe's were sketchy and allusive, at best drawing comparisons between their experiences. When Padre Brian spoke of his relationship with Anne, Joe seemed to follow with great interest, ready to seize upon any specifics that might bring Marianne back to mind. But the two stories were really quite different, and Joe remained reticent about revealing too much of himself. Padre Brian accepted that as he continued to relate his own tale.

During his last year at the university, Brian grew very close to Anne. To the amazement of many, they became a couple. They spent endless hours talking to one another. They studied together, though they majored in different subjects. As soon as they had some free time, they would borrow a car from a friend and head west for the mountains, where beautiful valleys stretched out and reddish peaks loomed over green forests. They were in love and enjoyed their discreet and tentative sexual encounters.

But as Padre Brian recounted their activities, it became clear that for young Brian, though he did not disdain sex, it was not the main reason for having a relationship with a woman.

For Joe it was the opposite: the physical bond in a relationship was very important, but he made no mention of this to the priest—he didn't want to stand on the other side of the river, as it were, and make conversation more difficult.

When Brian had completed his senior year, he returned to New Jersey, where he had been offered an excellent job. Although Anne had two more years before graduation, they decided to pursue their relationship.

In the beginning they wrote to one another frequently, and later somewhat less. They took two more trips to the mountains together. Then she went to see him in New Jersey. The next time around, he went to meet her in Seattle, where her family lived.

Things appeared to go well enough, but as time went on, the distance between them began to intrude and a mist descended between them. As it grew thicker, it blocked from view the bridge that had united them.

Or so Padre Brian described their increasing separation. When it came time to recount the last time they were together, the silences between his sentences grew and he refused to meet Joe's eyes.

It seemed to Joe that there was a great deal more to the break-up than Padre Brian was willing to say.

That feeling became confirmed when the Jesuit explained without emotion that he found out many years later that Anne had married, settled in Seattle, and had two children. Nothing more remained between them but brief bits of news and a few old photos.

Joe nonetheless had the impression that Padre Brian had to force himself to recall all these memories, which were by now so distant from his daily life.

Why, then, couldn't he place his recollections of Marianne on some back shelf of memory, the way Padre Brian did?

The Castaway

10

When Padre Brian and Joe visited the kindergarten, as they did often, it seemed that the Jesuit took particular care in making sure that Joe spent time with Sara. He often left him alone to help her with work that needed to be done around the compound.

Joe wasn't very good at manual jobs—in fact, he was quite clumsy—but he enjoyed doing them and tried to accomplish them with as few disasters as possible.

Joe had never met a woman like Sara, certainly not when he had been in college. He found her to be quite unusual and exotic, and she did not conform to his image of a typical director of a children's center. She had a great sense of humor. Her eyes shone with intense good cheer and often sparkled with curiosity.

But there were also times when, watching her closely without her noticing, Joe had the sensation, and later the certainty, that behind her attractive, open face and spontaneous and generous manner, there lurked great sadness. He understood that her strength was the ability to keep that sadness to herself while she encouraged others around her to partake in the pleasure of living.

Joe wondered if even in the game of sex she would perhaps act the same way.

He found himself interested in her—he wanted to find out what was behind Sara's bright green eyes—and the physical stirrings affected how he was willing to think about himself and his situation.

But who was he, at that moment, in that place, to allow himself the luxury of such questions and feelings?

If he were being honest with himself, he was just Joe the castaway, with a thousand problems and no solutions.

Yet, Sara's example unlocked something inside him. A little at a time he allowed memories to begin to take shape and color in his mind. Perhaps he could find the courage to resume his old lifestyle, own his passions and accept the sadness of his past.

Perhaps there was still a part of life worth living.

For the first time he considered the possibility that he could go back to using his real name, the name connected to his original identity, albeit in a different form, one forged by his new experiences.

He grew increasingly eager to learn about the life of Brian Christopher, the financial analyst, and how he had become Padre Brian. Perhaps the story of the Jesuit's transformation would provide an answer to his own difficulties. He wanted to make sure that what he considered a kind of rebirth for himself was real, in order to become confident enough to return to Florida, where he had begun his disastrous voyage.

Thus, he was happy to quench his thirst for meaning at Padre Brian's fountain of knowledge and wisdom.

As his conversations with the Jesuit deepened, Joe had the feeling that the man was concealing something from him inside his soul, some monumental event that had induced him to change lifestyles.

What had persuaded him to become a Jesuit? What's more, what was it that had driven him to estaablish a new life so far from his birthplace?

Usually Jesuits lived in communities, schools, universities; they belonged to well-defined organizations. But not Padre Brian. He himself seemed to provide the structure for all the activities that surrounded him.

In fact, it was very difficult to understand the relationships he carried on with both the Order and his benefactors. He had a broad network of people that helped support his activities, and he spent a good deal of time on the computer and on the telephone with them—speaking and writing in English, Spanish, French and Italian, as the case required. What seemed to interest him most was defending his own autonomy, since it was only in this way that he could dedicate himself fully to his job of helping people.

His office was large and well equipped; it had everything he needed. But most of all, it marked the boundaries of his personal realm.

If Joe wanted to talk to Padre Brian during the day, he usually knocked on the door and waited for permission to enter this "private" space. Then he moved with much caution amid the desks, shelves, computers, photocopier and fax machine. He had the impression he encountered another Brian there—the efficient businessman from New Jersey.

Joe stayed in the office no longer than he had to, as the most vital place for their intimacy was the living room.

Mornings, Padre Brian rose at dawn and went to say mass or to pray somewhere. Later he would inform Joe as to what activities he had planned for the day.

Evenings, if they didn't dine out, they went back home and cooked. Sometimes they read or watched television—the latter only for the time necessary to catch up on the latest news of the world. But mostly, they talked. And talked. And talked some more.

During the day, a middle-aged woman took care of the house, did the laundry and filled the refrigerator with the necessary provisions. If Padre Brian were in his office, the two exchanged a few words in Spanish, always in a cheerful, affectionate tone.

Practically speaking, most of Brian's time was absorbed in making his activities to assist others ever more functional and productive.

Sunday was different. Then Padre Brian dedicated himself to the duties his religion imposed upon him, which he carried out with great devotion and serenity. Indeed, for a few hours a week he became a real priest.

This alternating arrangement interested our castaway more and more as time went on. Indeed, he came to understand that one of Padre Brian's personal challenges was getting the three distinct personalities that were at war within his soul to co-exist peacefully: The man with the instinct to explore new horizons, the priest obliged to follow the catechism and its rules, and the Jesuit who, with his culture and training, could see both sides and wanted to create a synergy between the two that would project the whole toward a broader, more illuminated vision of the world.

He would often exclaim, "Easier said than done, and the goal is hard to reach, with more and more questions begging for answers—but that's how you hold yourself back. Good God! You know you exist, so get moving!"

Our castaway found it more and more difficult to be called Joe with each passing day. He was driven by Padre Brian's words to relive those moments of his former life in which he forced himself to at least come up with the right question, even if he had given up on determining a satisfactory answer.

One evening he mustered his courage and said, "My real name is Albert."

Padre Brian's reply was just as laconic. "I know."

The castaway was surprised, "You mean to tell me that you figured Joe wasn't my real name?"

"No. I meant exactly what I said. I was almost certain your name was Albert. I was wondering for a few days when you would confirm it." The Jesuit grinned. "Should I tell you your last name, too?"

"I know my last name. Maybe you know it because I said it in my sleep."

"No. The information showed up among a list of missing persons from the west coast of Florida. No one ever imagined in your hometown that you'd been lost at sea. No one knew about you setting sail in a catamaran until a few days ago, when by chance it was discovered that you bought one with cash. I've been keeping my eye on you, but I didn't want to make any false moves. I was waiting for you to tell me.

49

In the meantime, I have contacted your friends and your secretary, begging them to put off making the news public, in the hope that you would decide to officially remember what you've never forgotten.

You only wanted to escape, you were confused.

You needed time to answer, within yourself, a few simple questions.

By the way, don't worry—everything's okay in Sarasota. Your house and your business are being taken care of."

Albert reacted with a jolt of rebellion when confronted with this reality. His expression grew serious, but he said nothing.

Padre Brian handed him a glass of scotch, saying, "Have a seat. You can't run away from life. You've got to pursue it with seriousness and serenity in order to get out of it as much as you can, and to soothe your ever-restless spirit."

Albert obeyed like a scolded child and sat. At the same time, he felt freed of an enormous burden.

The moment had come to live the "truth" and let this sham, which had grown so tedious and taxing, fall by the wayside.

The Castaway

11

The news that Joe the castaway, the man without memory, had unearthed his roots and revealed his real name circulated among the community like wildfire and was reported to the American Consulate and the local police.

Brian's reputation for his ability to get people to open their hearts, even those who had lost their memory, grew even more. Even for Sara, it was further confirmation of Padre Brian's skill, personal force and spirituality. He was a much more complete and knowledgeable person than he pretended to be.

And so it was that, at last, Albert called his office in Sarasota, his bank, and Jeff, his architect friend and business partner.

The conversations were filled with emotion. Yet nothing seemed to have changed there. Albert found himself saying over and over again, "Everything's all right, I'm here, I'll be back, I'll get myself organized…send me money."

He signed some papers, and people on both sides of the Gulf of Mexico patiently awaited a decision from him.

His secretary sent several articles about him that appeared in the Sarasota newspapers. He read them with little interest and was pleased only that they were fairly vague. She also caught him up on what had happened at his firm in his absence. Fortunately, she and Jeff both had power of attorney, so with regard to Albert's own business dealings, they had been able to manage without him.

"Now what am I supposed to do?" Albert wondered.

It was a nagging question, but he lost no sleep over it. Nor did it upset the quiet flow of his everyday routine.

He had the feeling he was waiting for something to happen. But what?

Padre Brian seemed to think that the lifestyle Albert had assumed in the Yucatan had created a sort of safety net for him, and that it was necessary to leave him in peace so that he might regain his desire to cope with reality and re-engage with his former life.

For his part, Albert felt somewhat ill at ease with Padre Brian, who almost certainly knew too much about his personal life already. And the mystery that the priest seemed to be concealing troubled him as well.

Instead, he found a new confidante in Sara. She seemed like the perfect person for him: She was patient, but also determined and frank.

As a woman, and a beautiful one at that, she inspired in him a feeling of romantic melancholy.

While Padre Brian appeared surprised and delighted that Albert was spending so many hours with Sara, it was actually all part of his plan for Albert's recovery. He also hoped that their encounters would provide Sara with a stimulus that might reconnect her to her own previous existence.

He knew that they talked a great deal while they worked together, and that it did both of them good.

Sara and Albert spoke often about Padre Brian and agreed that, while he was an exceptional person, he was not an easy man. He seemed to emanate a strange intensity which conveyed the impression that he could penetrate your brain, your bones, indeed, the core of your being. Like a rich banquet, it was better to take him in small doses if you wanted to succeed in appreciating and loving him – otherwise you ran the risk of indigestion.

At Sara's prodding, Albert took a small house on the edge of town along the road to the kindergarten. She confirmed what he had begun to feel—that he did not want to take advantage of Padre Brian's hospitality. He pre-paid six months' rent.

Padre Brian understood the reason and supported his decision.

At Albert's invitation, the three often dined out together. But in time, more often than not, it was just Albert and Sara.

She showed considerable interest in the life of this strange castaway. Perhaps it was sparked by his initial stories, perhaps by his romantic spirit, or perhaps by the immediate attraction she'd felt at their very first meeting. Or maybe it was just female curiosity. In any case, in just a few days' time, through a series of disclosures masterfully elicited by Sara's questions, Albert told her about the critical moments of his life up until his shipwreck.

He described the years of his youth in Rhode Island, his untroubled relationship with his parents, his time at college where he earned a Bachelor's degree in international business, his life on Wall Street in the world of high finance and his business travels.

Then he reached the most important part – his love for Marianne, the woman he had married and whom fate had taken away, far away. But whereto?

Pressed by Sara, he described in detail the grueling metamorphosis that led to a new life—his work in Sarasota as a small construction entrepreneur, and his relationship with Joy, the woman he had left on the opposite shores of the Gulf of Mexico.

That fateful day, when he had set sail with the small catamaran, he had had the feeling he was leaving time behind and racing toward a place where he would meet Marianne. It was more than just a sensation, for he had lived those moments as if they were as real as Sara sitting in front of him now.

After being rescued by the merchant ship, he had refused to remember anything so that he would remain as long as possible in that state of timelessness, in which he would surely see Marianne once again.

Sara and Albert were both so moved by his account that they hugged each other like a brother and sister reunited after a long time apart.

That emotional moment was the result of a growing realization of change in both of their lives. Such a moment doesn't last long, and in their case, it left behind a sense of uncertainty and emptiness.

At the same time, comparisons between the newly recovered reality and lingering memories of the past raised a series of doubts and questions about one another.

After some initial confusion, Albert became curious why Sara had become so emotional in identifying with his story about Marianne. He knew that Sara was a generous woman whose deep eyes offered serenity and hope. But why did they also convey such an intense sense of sadness emanating from deep within?

What had brought her to seek voluntary exile from the world by working as a principal of a kindergarten here in a quiet corner of the Yucatan peninsula?

Albert, newly resuscitated, didn't know what his next move should be.

This enigmatic woman, who had such a frank, straightforward manner and powerful sexuality, which she tried to conceal with little success, fascinated him; but he couldn't explain where her powerful allure came from. Furthermore, he didn't know whether he should reveal his attraction for her. He wanted to, but he didn't feel ready to act while he still carried so many burdens of his previous life. He certainly didn't want to add to her sadness with his own.

Sara, for her part, found herself in a state of growing apprehension generated by Albert's re-emergence to present-day reality. Instead of being "Joe the castaway," someone to be pitied, he now assumed a real and concrete status for her. In his new role he was a complex man, haunted and obsessed by the past, who could also be charming, sensitive and quite appealing.

It was complicated. The name had changed, but Sara didn't know what that meant, and she was afraid to examine her heart and open herself up to him. She had made such poor choices in relationships with men in the past. Could she trust herself to do better this time?

Was Albert really different or just another version of the same heartbreakers, albeit in a pleasant disguise?

And yet, perhaps also for Sara, the time was right to awaken from her voluntary exile from the world at large.

And so they maintained a zone of safety between them during their frequent meetings. In the meantime, Sara carried on in her routines as principal of the kindergarten, and Albert continued to help Padre Brian, as they both longed to awaken from their own self-imposed hibernation.

The Castaway

12

One day Albert decided he had to return to Florida. It came to him all of a sudden, and he acted without giving it a second thought and without discussing it with Sara or Padre Brian.

He left his clothes and the few objects he had bought in the little house he had rented.

It was only after having checked in at the airport that he decided to call all those involved, both in Mexico and the United States, and inform them that he was returning to Sarasota.

In Miami he rented a car and headed west, glad to get away from that part of Florida that he always felt was not North America, nor South America, nor Europe, but only chaos.

Driving along the monotonous stretch of highway called Alligator Alley, which crosses the peninsula like the trajectory of a bullet, he began to feel a bit apprehensive. He was getting closer to home—the home he had left so hastily, with no plan, no agenda, just chasing a dream, or rather, a vision. He did not regret fleeing, but he was feeling just a bit uncomfortable over all the problems it may have caused for many people.

He had acted like a naughty schoolboy playing hooky.

At a certain point, Alligator Alley curved in a soft and wide arc. He hadn't remembered that. Everything wasn't flat and straight in the middle of Florida after all.

He drove up the west coast past Naples and Venice, once again amused at the penchant of Americans to give their communities names that take them back to the roots of their European descendants and legitimize the origin of their culture.

When he started to see the signs for Sarasota, he thought, "My escape is over and I have come full circle. Do I know something more?" The question remained without answer.

He had to exit the highway and drive west on Fruitville Road toward the Gulf of Mexico. He called the office and had a nice chat with his secretary and a few words with Jeff who said, "Go directly to your place. I will be there to open the door. I'm sure you don't have the keys with you."

Approaching the familiar buildings downtown, he had a feeling that he was coming back to a friendly place. Although, he was not so sure that he could call it home anymore without qualifications.

He still had strong feelings for Rhode Island, where he had spent his youth, and for New York, where he met Marianne.

After they had married, they intended for Sarasota to become their permanent residence, and it did for a while, until she went back to New York for an appointment on that terrible day of September 11, 2001 and didn't return.

He had stayed on, trying to find a reason to live, or rather to survive. He had moved from their house to a condo that he now could see up ahead.

As he approached the building, he started to fantasize, as he had done all these years since, asking himself the impossible: Could Marianne be there? Perhaps she was waiting to open the door to his condo. But she never lived there. How could she know where he moved to...?

He gripped the steering wheel and berated himself, "Stop. Stop fantasizing! You've done this so many times, but ... but this time you know better.

You have learned a lot of lessons; you have accumulated too many experiences.

Open your eyes to new realities and new friendships that penetrate deep inside you. Don't play this game again.

Think about Jeff, the architect, a friendly and honest person with whom you share a small construction business. Think about Gregg, even if he is not your cup of tea with his unpleasant character. Your friendship was founded after that quarrel he had with Joy at the restaurant, and they split up...and she ended up in your bed. Joy, a strange woman, who with her strong and twisted character, helped cement your friendship with Gregg and practically gave you the excuse to go sailing in the Gulf of Mexico."

As he had imagined, his arrival sparked delight and a certain amount of curiosity. During his first days back, he was subjected to some inquiries, but they were few and asked with the utmost discretion. When he gave vague answers, they soon ceased. As far as the media went, his story wasn't all that interesting—he had been lost at sea and rescued by a ship—and rated only a small notice in the local papers and a brief mention on the television news.

After a few days, though, he felt like he'd never been away, and he fell back into his old routines. He dined at the usual spots where he saw his friends again. He had lunch with Gregg, and they even talked a bit about Joy. She was the only person Albert didn't want to see, because she would bombard him with questions he didn't want to answer. So he kept her at bay by having friends spread the news that he had no intention of meeting with her. When she tried to call him, he refused to answer. After a few times, she apparently gave up and left him in peace.

Alone in his apartment, he felt as isolated as before.

What had happened was something that had happened to him and him alone, and desperately.

No one could understand what he'd gone through on the open sea. No one but Marianne, and she was no longer there for him. However, on second thought, that was not true. There were others involved now in all he had experienced. How could he just dismiss the many hours spent talking with Padre Brian, and the emotionally intense times with Sara?

But all that belonged to another world, those two people were no longer a part of his regular routine. They were too far away to affect his life. And yet…

What was all this foolishness?

Of course those people were important to him!

Actually, he couldn't stop thinking about Sara and the Jesuit.

It didn't matter that they lived on the other side of the Gulf of Mexico. Between them, separating them, lay only that stretch

of blue water, which sometimes turned exquisite turquoise in the sun.

He had already overcome that barrier once with a simple catamaran, without really knowing what he was doing. Now he knew where to land.

What's more, he knew how to overcome the distance —there were telephones, airplanes, cars and ships. What wonderful inventions! They truly brought people together. He had never thought that before.

He longed to hear news from them, but they did not call.

Impatient, Albert decided to call them himself. He picked up the receiver.... Sara answered, with that special lilt in her voice that revealed the simplicity of her soul and the openness of her heart.

He thought he heard a note of surprise, though. Not all that many days had passed since he'd left them. She and Padre Brian had decided not to call him, figuring that he needed time to himself.

They chattered on about practically nothing—normal exchanges regarding everyday life, the weather, and a few pointed questions about Padre Brian. Albert asked her to tell the Jesuit that he would call him in two or three days. The conversation ended quickly.

But when Albert hung up the phone, he felt a sense of deep-rooted melancholy, issuing from the depth of his soul and slowly transmuting into a feeling of serenity.

The Castaway

13

For the next few days, Albert tried to put his life in order and get back to work. But he soon realized that all he was doing was checking on his investments, crunching numbers and adopting strategies that would preserve his investments and wealth. It was all so familiar, yet it left him cold. He did not really care about the office, or his brief period dabbling in construction, or the plans he'd made and projects his architect friend hoped to undertake.

Living in the quagmire of rules that American bureaucracy was becoming, even at a local level, was stifling as ever, and it constricted his soul.

Years earlier, when he had worked in Europe, each time he returned to the States he felt as if reborn. He wondered how people on the old continent could realize, with joy and profit, any work plan at all. They were forced to operate within a system that overflowed with all the complications created by an old, but well-oiled bureaucratic machine, held in place by a political system that did its best to obscure social realities. Officially it had to give the appearance of being socialist, or rather populist, while at the same time it created opportunities in the world of business and finance that were accessible to an extremely limited number of people—always the same elite.

Unfortunately, in recent years, America had taken to imitating the complexities of European bureaucracy even if it did so based on more straightforward and practical logic than false social considerations. The difference lay in the fact that Americans would not easily give up what they believed to be their rights as citizens. This led them to wage legal battles which created a vicious cycle of lawsuits and countersuits. This in turn provided work for a mass of lawyers, consultants, journalists and other unscrupulous figures who, once they understood the mechanism, prospered by giving false hopes and clever remedies.

Old-time businessmen who still remembered the years gone by—which in reality were not so very long ago—coined the phrase, "What used to be easy has grown difficult, what used to be difficult has become impossible."

The only positive thing that Albert saw in the United States was that these cycles of economic and emotional depression, created by excessive bureaucratic interference, alternated fairly frequently with cycles of enthusiasm, which tended to sweep away most of the constraints.

This was an aspect that Europe, static in its convictions, could not manage to comprehend.

At any rate, his experience in an area of Mexico that suffered under a particularly fastidious bureaucratic system, worse than anything he had experienced before, had intensified in him the perception of this aspect of society, which for him had become too confining and crippling.

Bureaucracy in Mexico was enormous, inefficient, and the country's politics were a madcap adventure, but people there adapted to it because there was no proficient economic system that worked as well as the American.

In the United States, things could go very badly, but not for long. After a certain period, people driven by the common will to react put their minds to work to find a solution to the problem. In Mexico, efficiency had not yet been invented.

Albert had found the attitude of many Mexicans extraordinary. Even if everything had been made difficult, one could remain indifferent in the face of so many obstacles and seek to live—live and nothing more.

On the other hand, these problems posed no obstacle to Albert when he worked only with capital.

Money, when it comes down to it, has no flag, no boss, no fixed domicile; money is extremely mobile—everyone is interested in it, everyone wants it, especially small-minded people that rail against it in the name of fairness and justice. Money follows well-drawn channels which, if managed with care and prudence, keep one safe from most major mishaps.

Without the expenses of a family, Albert still had significant capital, which, if administered correctly, would be enough to provide him with everything he needed. In the Yucatan, that kind of income could procure him a life of leisure, that was for sure.

All of this became clear to Albert when sitting at the office, listening to his partner explain what had happened during his absence and expound on future projects. What stuck in his mind the most was not the difficulty of designing and building a good, salable product and finding the financing, but the continuous and tedious problems created by the bureaucratic machine. At best it was interested in making people miserable and causing damage it didn't care about. The funny thing was that in the end, everything worked out, but at a tremendous cost of time, money and stress, which took away the joy of the work. And if the drive disappeared, it could lead to economic disaster.

He performed such reasoning not because he longed to leave America. These were merely considerations which unconsciously led him to call Sara at least once a day, and Padre Brian twice a week.

Hearing her voice soothed his sense of deprivation, and while their conversations seemed to be mostly about mundane and ordinary things, they grew closer with each call.

The philosophical and sometimes poetic discussions with Padre Brain made him forget the feelings of unhappiness and lack of fulfillment in his heart. But the priest also dug into his intimate self with his increasingly appropriate and shrewd observations. Perhaps, besides being a man, priest and a Jesuit, he was also something of a devil—a good devil, and rather unconventional in his views on relationships, in order to encourage Sara's and Albert's growing intimacy.

And so Sara's role grew within Albert's psyche, as if it were a theater in which Sara moved from ingénue to leading lady. In contrast, Padre Brian seemed to slip backstage, like a director who, having finished staging a play, watches it from the wings while waiting to be called in for his next assignment.

The Castaway

Sara came to Sarasota.

There had been much talk in the past, much discussion of life's values, and the responsibilities and relationships that bound people together, but they all seemed to be blown in the breeze, the sea breeze that caressed the terrace of Albert's apartment.

It must have been three in the afternoon, the sun was shining. The bedroom was just off the terrace.

What they had never admitted out loud might happen one day, because they wanted to preserve their profound friendship, happened in an instant.

Neither spoke for hours, overcome by the irresistible urge to just find one another, discover and touch one another, delight in one another and relish one another, suffer, become young again, forget ... in short, a day so good that they could go back to dreaming and fantasizing.

PART II

THE JESUIT

The Castaway

14

Sitting in his usual armchair in the study of his modest home, Padre Brian had fallen into a profound state of sadness. His spirit was roaming over desolate and often agonizing paths. For many years, after having become a priest, and a Jesuit at that, when his mind was caught up in such thoughts, he felt lost and figured the only solution was either to bury himself in his work or pour himself a glass of scotch in dire need to forget.

Earlier he had received a telephone call from Albert and Sara. They'd sounded happy, traveling around Europe, and currently enjoying a cruise to the Greek islands.

Hearing their voices had provided him with a moment's distraction. He was glad for them. In his mind, for a few minutes, he traveled among the ancient Greek myths, whose gods, so real and human, were still able to fascinate and allure. But that was just a brief interlude, and he soon returned to his mood of dejection.

He wondered if Albert had managed to put his obsession over Marianne's disappearance out of his mind.

He had followed his intuition when he accompanied poor Joe, who had lost his memory, to the kindergarten to meet Sara. He thought all those children and a young woman with an American culture might help him break free from the memory-loss alibi he was hiding behind. But then, observing their behavior, an almost obsessive idea took hold of his conscious thought: Sara and Joe.

When he later learned Joe's true identity and of the tragedy of Marianne, he became even more convinced that he must encourage this new relationship. They were both sensitive and profound people who had gone through a lot, at least as far as their sentiments were concerned.

He was glad to see Albert and Sara forge an alliance and provide reciprocal comfort as they overcame their past together. He knew all about Sara's past which, while not as dramatic as Albert's or his own, could definitely be considered confused and without focus.

Sara had suffered a great deal from the separation of her parents, whose different temperaments had made divorce inevitable. She had reacted by traveling widely, immersing herself in different cultures, and learning different languages. But she had never felt on solid ground, and her love life had always been wracked with disappointment, probably due to the depth of her sentiments. In search of something uncommon, something special, she had made bad decisions in her relationships with men.

Her job as director of the kindergarten under the protective wing of Padre Brian had had a healing effect and offered her a new direction, a foundation that would allow her to build a bright future for herself in line with her abilities, her intelligence and her charm.

Because of their respective pasts, she and Albert might not be able to feel the power of true love conjoined with passion, but they could experience the joy of sincere, soothing pleasure in being together.

Padre Brian had not been able to find such a solution in his own life. He had gone from what he called "love-passion," which he kept locked in his heart, to "love-devotion," which had led to his religious calling. He had not been born a Jesuit, much less a priest.

Love-passion and love-devotion—both difficult and exhausting conditions. He could not say if one was more demanding than the other, but he had no desire to see these two people caught up in either.

To be sure, his own experience with love-passion had not been the university adventure he told Albert about. Actually, he had to work to remember the details of that love affair. He had recounted it to show Albert that he too could talk about certain experiences in the field of male-female relations and to help him reconnect with the world. But the relationship that had changed his life forever, he had continued to keep a secret.

That thought led him to consider how sometimes, demons exist inside us, which we ourselves have created. They torment our existence and destroy any chance of delighting in the joy that may derive from the good experiences we have had, even if life carries with it an inevitable dose of disillusion and pain.

This was something he knew all too well.

While nurturing Albert and Sara's relationship was part of the routine duty of the life that Padre Brian had dedicated himself to, a life of helping others, Brian the man had not sufficiently evaluated his own, shall we say "spiritual" relationship with Sara.

Seeing her gave him great pleasure, lent meaning to his day. Her smile and those eyes of hers, so deep and intense, brought him back to that period of his life which he had so jealously kept hidden. Her refined ways, her delicate, supple movements, became a part of his existence.

He knew good and well that he was an old-timer, and, what's more, a priest loaded down with commitments. But when it wafts through the air, no one is prohibited from perceiving the scent of pretty things—a privilege not to be refused.

This is certainly no sin, but a hymn in praise of God-given life.

All too often, the evolution of events causes this scent to disperse, just when we have lulled ourselves into thinking it would be there forever.

In introducing Albert to Sara, and fostering their friendship, Padre Brian had unconsciously set this process into motion, and provoked a reaction that came from the darkest, most concealed part of a person. This reaction at first appears uncontrollable and usually generates the doubt, "What have you done? You've deprived yourself of something which gave you pleasure, and you've given it to someone else, forgetting all about yourself and your natural jealousy."

Reason's counter-reaction is simple enough to imagine: "Enjoy the good you seek to do, savor your decision to give love with the aim of creating new love. Perform this redeeming act so that it may set into motion a new process of life and love. Hope that you may represent something positive for the future.

Indeed, you may only hope in the positive effects of your actions, since it is impossible to know whether the friendship they embody will be a true blessing or a cause of other problems."

The ping-pong effect of these thoughts was enough to put even a Jesuit like Padre Brian on edge. He had to keep it all hidden from Albert and Sara, although he suspected that Sara, with her sensitive nature and women's intuition, had probably guessed as much. And even Albert may have picked up some of the signs.

Still, no one knew for certain that he harbored such thoughts.

Here in the Yucatan, he was known only as a great benefactor, a man with the glow of sainthood about him.

Many people took note of his unconventional methods, but there was always an explanation and excuse for them: His efficiency and goodness performed this miracle every day.

People no longer cared whether he was a saint, a devil, a man, a priest or a Jesuit. His deeds spoke for him. But when evening came and he was alone, sometimes memories of his past overwhelmed him.

That had been especially true the past few evenings. Perhaps because of Albert and Sara's calls, he had reverted to reflecting on his memories of that nightmarish period that led him to join the Jesuit Order.

Once the important decision regarding his new religious life was made, all the experiences that followed came as a direct consequence, an ongoing attempt to balance his chosen calling with his natural temperament, and to tend to his soul, which had been marked by the events.

His faith in life's positive nature was unshakable. He persisted in the conviction that a good quantity of love exists in each of us, and if it is not evident, it should be sought out and set free; and that commitment to helping others was the key to unlocking it and allowing him to travel the golden path with intensity.

Intensity and determination led to the rediscovery of love. It was necessary. But to do so required surmounting the tricks and hurdles put in the way by the legal, politico-bureaucratic system and its visionless plodding.

It demanded effort to seek out practicality in life and restore the proper measure of things, to rediscover a way of thinking and acting with simplicity. But it was possible by learning to apply two words which nowadays seem so antiquated, worn out, mocked and out of fashion: "common sense." In truth, common sense is something that people carry at the bottom of their souls. If they only stopped for a moment, listened to it, used it and spread it around.

We can cultivate our dreams and illusions, which are an important part of our existence, but they belong to us alone, and we are the only ones who may revel in them and cherish them. It is also up to us to control them so that they can be channeled, allowing us to escape, yet making a quick return to everyday reality when necessary.

That evening, Padre Brian felt a vague desire that seemed to be on the verge of becoming concrete.

"Enough!" he heard himself repeating. "Enough! After so many years I must find someone to tell my story to. I've buried it in daily routine, marked by the passing of so many months and years that they seem like minutes on the face of a clock. But to

what end? I must be able to tell it to someone, describe in detail the encounters and vicissitudes which, after that fateful night, led me to embark upon a new career as a Jesuit."

He thought that this story should not die with him and remain suffocated for ever. It had to come out in the open; it had to serve to generate in others some kind of emotion to reflect upon. Maybe it could help someone else, too, by clearing up a little confusion about life.

Wasn't that so?

Didn't all our deepest stories share that possibility?

"Padre Brian, be honest," he heard himself once again. "Padre Brian, be honest…Padre Brian, be honest with yourself. You just want to transfer your burden onto others, don't you? You want the world to take part in your grand crusade for redemption. You want to lighten your heart and show others that you are a human being, and one that has been injured to boot. Show yourself exactly the way you are, not the great generous and proficient man who does all he can to help others. You just want someone to feel sorry for you and to cry with you!"

He remained silent and immobile in his armchair, as if frightened by the thought. Then he rose and walked gravely toward the bedroom. In the doorway, he looked at the crucifix hanging on the wall above his bed and said out loud, "Why not? I'm a man, too…just a simple man."

But unlike his normal, energetic stride, he seemed to be dragging his feet—or at least that was the sensation he had—accompanied by the acrid smell of old age.

The Castaway

15

It was a day of gusty wind, which chased large white clouds of every shape across the clear blue sky. Most of them were forming round spirals that hovered here and there. In between, portions of the sky were at times even blinding, depending on where you looked, because the sun in that part of the world is always a powerful force and finds a way to grab attention, even when the day is overcast.

Padre Brian had stopped by the kindergarten and stayed a little longer than usual. The noise of the children cheered him. Actually, his recent patience with children amazed him. Many times in the past, after just a few minutes, he would begin to hear a buzzing inside his head and make up an excuse to get back in his car and drive through the open fields toward the main road.

But as the years passed, he had begun to feel grandfatherly, and his way of appreciating all aspects of life had changed.

There was, however, another reason, he had to admit.

The place brought to mind Sara—with her youthful and fresh thoughts, and her mature, capable ways of handling day-to-day problems. The memory of her in turn brought to mind that first day again when he'd brought Albert, who was still Joe the castaway then, to the kindergarten to meet the director he admired so and who always had a smile for him.

He wasn't quite sure anymore why he had done that. The excuse was to get a reaction out of the poor fellow who had lost his memory and try to reawaken him, or at least find a way to ferret out his secret.

Perhaps, though, there was something else that had pushed him to drive Joe the road that led to the kindergarten.

He did not want to admit it at the time, he couldn't.

He was a priest, and a fairly old one at that, with a bagful of sadness that would have made Sara lose her smile for good had he shared his burden with her.

Perhaps Joe...perhaps Joe could make something blossom anew in her—impossible for Padre Brian...perhaps Padre Brian would be happy to see them smile together...perhaps it had only to do with Sara...he was a priest, but he was also a man...perhaps he wished to hurt himself...perhaps he wanted Sara to fly away.

"What idiotic thoughts," he huffed as he got out of the car. He greeted the new director, who met him at the front door, with a relaxed expression on her face. In contrast to Sara, she was a heavy-set, matronly woman, but she was just as competent in her own way.

She smiled pleasantly at him and said, "It looks like we're going to be having visitors today." She pointed to a car slowly heading toward them. Padre Brian noticed something odd: It was clean, almost shiny, unlike all the other cars in the village.

Now and then, the car would slow down, then speed up and slow down again, as if the occupants were looking for something or paying special attention to some detail of the scenery that caught their eyes.

"That car's a bit out of place round these parts," said Padre Brian, not really knowing why he'd said it.

He felt a strange premonition in his heart.

Could it be them?

It was.

As the car pulled into the compound, he could see Albert behind the wheel and Sara next to him in the passenger seat.

Cheerfully smiling, they got out of the car and dispensed their happiness and carefree manner to the children that immediately swarmed around them—like a gift from some far-away, exotic part of the world.

For a moment, Padre Brian did not know what to say and could not understand what emotion had filled him up.

He had been waiting for this moment without admitting it to himself. But now with them standing there smiling before him, he grew flustered. A shiver ran down his spine and he wondered, once again, whether the union he had been instrumental in creating would lead to good or engender further complication and pain.

He had played at being God. He had sought to create an antidote for life's frustrations, and he was almost afraid to look at what he had wrought. Besides, like all antidotes, this one too would last a limited time only. Then what?

He willed the thoughts from his mind, forced himself to overcome his hesitation and opened his arms to embrace first Sara, then Albert.

After the initial exchange of enthusiastic greetings and easy laughter, the conversation became a bit awkward. All three stood there, feeling somewhat overwhelmed by the situation. There were the children, the kindergarten and all its memories, the new director, the past personified by the new arrivals and the spiritually reassuring figure of the Jesuit.

Memories of the past and unspoken hopes, expectations and aspirations for the future.

It was too much! Too much to communicate!

Padre Brian broke the ice and excused himself – he had errands to run in town, chores to perform. The visitors understood and were relieved as well.

Albert smiled graciously and said, "Of course, why don't you come to my place when you are finished. We'll have lunch."

The Castaway

16

On their way back to the house, Sara and Albert bought groceries. As they unpacked and settled in, they remained quiet, both focusing inwardly on personal thoughts.

Soon, the Jesuit arrived. The three gathered in the small kitchen and talked, catching up on what had happened since they'd last all been together. They kept their conversation superficial and on conventional topics as they prepared a quick lunch together.

Thanks to his acute perception skills, which he kept well hidden beneath his gruff outer layer, Padre Brian realized that it was up to him to break the ice.

He started to test the waters by inquiring, "So tell me about yourselves. Where have you been, how's life been treating you?"

It took a certain effort on his part to squelch his desire to ask outright whether the two were married or had plans to do so. He had looked for wedding bands on their hands, but hadn't seen any. So he held his curiosity in check. It would have looked as if he were putting too much emphasis on his priestly role in wanting everything to be proper, as it should be.

He did wonder, though, what "as it should be" meant in this case? Maybe it was what religion and the law dictated, or what God apparently appreciated within the human spirit: honesty, goodness, love. All too often, religion and laws did not agree with the message of love that is handed out in the name of God. This had always been the point at which his thoughts crashed like waves upon the rocks and he was overcome by confusion.

Still, the afternoon was pleasant and went by quickly. Sara and Albert filled Padre Brian in on many events in their lives and travels. But while they related many adventures and personal experiences, they were wary not to discuss any details of their more intimate moments together.

All three realized that the reason behind their prudence was not merely a sense of decency with regard to talking to a priest, but that there was something more delicate involving their relationship, something more intimate between them which sharpened their sensitivity and tied their tongues.

He sensed that they wanted to share something with him, but they either could not or would not say what it was. Who knew if perhaps one day they would be able to overcome their reluctance?

Surely, only when that moment had arrived would Padre Brian's soul be freed of a great burden. And Sara and Albert would be freed from their sense of embarrassment and guilt with regard to the good Jesuit.

Padre Brian returned to his home troubled. The time spent with his friends kept occupying his thoughts.

He had been glad to see that Sara and Albert appeared at ease with each other—it was the thing that counted for him. But as the conversation had proceeded, he had sensed that there was still some distance between them, despite the surface happiness, an undercurrent of something that their travels together had not been able to resolve. Perhaps Albert still had not fully escaped Marianne's "spiritual" hold, preventing him from committing to Sara with the fullness of his being, not just his physical presence. For Sara the fact that Albert was both similar and different from the men she had encountered in the past was weighing on her. For certain she asked herself: Was she involved with another man who carried only his problems with him and let them define him?

The Marianne situation certainly was a difficult one. Perhaps Sara had doubts that Albert was different enough to have things work out for a change.

Whatever the reasons were, Padre Brian felt that both of them were smoldering with a fire inside, fanned by a series of problems and misunderstandings that neither fully grasped. Unchecked, the flames would rage and at some point destroy everything good in their relationship. Of that he was certain.

It was well after midnight, but he couldn't bring himself to go to bed. He seemed stuck in his armchair, but he had the feeling that something important was churning in his mind, trying to break through to the surface. In the past, when that happened, it always felt like a miracle.

At some point, he rose decisively and said out loud, "Yes. I will tell my story to Albert and Sara, and in as much detail as possible. If it is a selfish act to unburden myself to them and share the pain in my heart, so be it! Yet I also believe that it will help clear up the situation between them and allow them to put their lives in order."

He started to walk toward his bedroom, but stopped abruptly once more. "Albert … Albert…put your love for Marianne where it belongs, in the box of memories.

Why don't you realize that everybody knows she died in New York on September 11?

Yes, the times with her were good and unforgettable, but they are just a memory! Albert, it's time to find a new life and to dedicate yourself to the present, not the past."

He went to bed, and for the few hours that remained before morning, he sank into a solid, deep sleep.

The Castaway

17

The miracle occurred a few days later.

It was late Sunday afternoon, the three of them were at Albert's house. The conversation began half-heartedly, over a cup of tea, then took on vigor, and became quite deep.

It was as if the three had wanted to bring out everything that was oppressing them, seeking a kind of spiritual purge that would cleanse the convolutions of the brain from the leftovers of previous, hard-to-digest thoughts. Such a purge may be but a brief, temporary remedy, though at times it is necessary, even if those involved know perfectly well that it will not last. But there is value in such moments of relief, and they are special. In truth, our lives are a sum of diverse moments lined up one after the other, and those considered important by society are, for the most part, tedious, while the ones we seek to keep all our own are by far more exciting.

Padre Brian could sense Sara and Albert's bewilderment and longing. At a certain point in their conversation he simply interjected, "When I was married..."

The words remained hanging in midair, as he stopped and looked up into their eyes—first Albert's, then Sara's. Suddenly he felt a surge of joy, as if an old burden of rancor had melted in his heart. He had an absurd thought—that it reminded him of the effect of two Alka-Seltzer tablets on the stomach after indigestion—and he chuckled.

"When I was married..." He'd actually said it!

He felt as if he were perched at the top of a rollercoaster, ready to take the ride of his life. He felt the need to talk and spill his secrets, with all their twists and turns, in a way he had never done before.

Sara, with a hint of a smile, said, "I didn't know. I'd figured you lived an intense life prior to becoming a Jesuit. It never dawned on me that you might have been married."

"Intense life?" Padre Brian quickly responded. "I have always lived a simple life, first as a student, then as a corporate manager and as a simple businessman, without many emotions to remember.

But one day I encountered love, absolute love.

It was an amazing discovery. The surprise...lasted a short while, but this was not due to boredom and apathy.

It was short-lived because fate or providence willed it so. Since then I've been racking my brains, asking myself what providence requires of us, and what it is in reality."

Albert followed the conversation very carefully. At a certain point he got up, agitated, and blurted out, "I knew it. I knew it! I figured your heart bore a scar of love. I imagined that beyond the light-weight college relationship you'd told me about, there had to be something else that had led you to make certain choices. The way you spoke to me, and your curiosity about what happened with Marianne… told me that you had experienced something similar. The way you looked at Sara, and how you encouraged me to spend time with her.

That was gratification for you, even if your sense of jealousy was aroused. But at least one of us had the opportunity to re-make destiny. I was available, and still had chances for success. You knew how to use me…"

"What are you talking about?" Padre Brian interrupted, having grown red in the face. "I did nothing but convince you to reconnect with the memories you hadn't lost, but refused to recognize."

"Enough of this bickering!" Sara suddenly exclaimed. She turned to Albert, "You're absolutely heartless. Don't you see that Padre Brian has found the strength to open his heart in order to soothe his pain?

And that he has chosen us to open up to?

I consider it a precious gift, one that shows great esteem for our spirits. Don't you?"

Sara hesitated for a moment and got herself under control before she continued. "After all he did for you, you want to take this joy away from him?

We ourselves have benefited from his long years of nurturing and tending to others, like trees whose fruit ripened with his love for mankind.

Are you taking back everything you've said to me these past few days?

Let him tell his life's story.

Give him the chance and listen.

That's the greatest gift we can bestow on him and offer in return for what he did for us. Learn to listen.

We have always listened to you. Even when you played at being absent-minded Joe."

Albert was on the verge of losing his temper, but in a flash he lowered his eyes. For a moment he looked like a dog who knows he has done something terribly wrong. Had he had a dog's pointy ears, he would have lowered them, too.

Padre Brian, hushed, seemed at a loss. His bright, clear eyes stared straight ahead. He looked as ready as ever to communicate, but it was obvious he did not know where to begin.

Sara came to the rescue. "Tell us your story," she urged. "It will do you good. It will also do me, and especially Albert, some good."

The Castaway

18

Padre Brian had been waiting a long time for this opportunity. Now there were two people sitting before him, ready to receive his "confession," willing to hear him out with affection—though Albert would listen with a somewhat critical spirit. But in the meantime, he had calmed down and seemed to want to move past what he had said in a moment of anger.

Padre Brian perceived their readiness to listen, and he began.

Back east, after graduating from college, he had gotten a job with a large distribution firm in New Jersey, as he had told Albert. He rose rapidly in the company. He was intelligent, diligent, he knew what to do with numbers and budgets, he possessed good organizational skills, and he did not disdain long working hours. He was also ready to travel whenever his job commitments required.

In his spare time, he played tennis, lunched at clubs with his friends, and attended concerts, operas and theater performances in New York. Life passed like a summer breeze, but while it was filled with activities, it lacked the spark that Brian's sensitive soul needed.

He often visited his parents, who were affectionate, pleasant and still full of life, but did not hide their concern over Brian's lifestyle—his intense workload and his lack of a solid relationship with a woman that might become his partner for life.

"Being two," they used to say, "can have its problems, but sharing your life with someone adds a rainbow of colors. And arguing actually helps love heighten moments of pleasure between disagreements."

Brian laughed and talked about it with them amiably enough, but their admonitions didn't seem to change his attitude. And while he occasionally went out on dates, he did not appear to show much interest in the joys that the opposite sex promised.

Then everything changed.

He was in Chicago for a conference. One evening, after he'd finally finished all his commitments, he went out to dinner with the manager of a company engaged in the same line of work as his. They'd known one another for several years and through their various business dealings had come to appreciate each other's company from time to time. Bob was older than Brian, but the two had similar ways of reasoning and dealing with problems. Brian enjoyed learning from the experience of a seasoned veteran, while Bob relished the opportunity to understand what direction the younger generation was taking—he did not want to feel he was becoming obsolete.

That evening, Bob brought his daughter Barbara along to dinner with him.

No ulterior motive, no special plan, just destiny.

She appeared to be at least five years younger than Brian, and the first thing he noticed was her dark eyes.

That evening, Brian felt a sense of uncontainable curiosity well up inside him—he had to find out everything about this woman. He wasn't all that much concerned about her past, but he felt compelled to ask her questions, to look at her, find out what lay behind those deep eyes of hers.

He was fascinated by the way she spoke and moved her lips, by her smile and by the way her nostrils flared when she got excited. When she got up to go to the ladies' room, Brian caught himself watching the shape and movement of her legs. As she returned to the table, he indulged in contemplating her bearing, especially the way her breasts moved beneath her blouse.

A self-reflective man, he was surprised and had to stop himself from saying out loud, "What kind of experience between the incredible and the idiotic am I having here?"

In reality, the young woman was not exceptionally beautiful, but she attracted Brian in a way he had never felt before.

Perhaps this was the kind of passion so many people long for, but few ever encounter.

His own limited experience did not help him to understand what he was feeling. Until he met Barbara, women had symbolized friendly, efficient companionship, and he had enjoyed sharing in their various abilities and attitudes. The encounters of beings from Mars and Venus, whose approaches to the problems of this world were so different, had brought him reasonable pleasure and fulfillment, or so he had thought.

But that evening, Brian felt the devastating effect a woman could have on a man like him, who was so measured in his approach to life and for whom work and business were everything.

It felt as if her dark eyes, so lively and profound, and her languid smile were meant just for him. When she talked, he felt her intense focus on him as if he were the only one in the restaurant.

"The unlucky girl," thought Brian, who did not see himself as a brilliant man or one particularly skilled in socializing. "Why should she be interested in me?"

But he could not take his eyes off her either. He was so enthralled with her that he hardly registered their conversation.

It turned out that Barbara was taking courses in New York—in some subject that escaped his notice. But the words "New York" rang out with the intense clarity of church bells on a crisp summer day.

She was living just a few miles from him!

All he had to do was cross the George Washington Bridge.

Padre Brian leaned back and took a sip of his tea. He let the silence settle, as if he were hesitant to tell what happened on the other side of the bridge.

Sara was the first to react. As she got up to refill everyone's cups, she said, "Why did you call her 'the unlucky girl,' just because she was attracted to you? You have always had too low a consideration of yourself. Believe me, she was very lucky."

Albert grimaced slightly. He didn't seem to appreciate Sara's comment or Padre Brian's reply, "You are always very kind."

But he was fascinated all the same and said, "I want to hear the end of the story."

Padre Brian noted his impatience and, with a wistful smile, continued his tale.

The Castaway

19

The next day, Brian flew back to Newark with Barbara's address in his pocket and, more importantly, with a promise to meet her when she returned to New York three days later. He resolved not to call her until the time they had agreed upon, although he was not sure whether this was the right attitude or whether he was being overly passive.

It was a long, tedious wait. Time slowed to a crawl for him. He felt like he was back in college, when days were like weeks and months like years. He counted the hours like a student who can't wait for the end of school, to be free to go out and explore the world.

The emptiness of the work routine seemed to stretch before him like a monotonous desert. What was happening to him?

The future Padre Brian, the man, the priest and the Jesuit, had come across a situation completely new to him. He was in the throes of what he called "love-passion" – deep affection and respect for the other combined with intense excitement and sexual longing.

They met on the other side of the George Washington Bridge, in midtown Manhattan. Brian remembered leaving his car in a large parking garage, then taking a taxi to pick up Barbara and going to a restaurant on the Upper East Side between 3rd and Lexington Avenue. While he had forgotten the address and the name, he still recalled every detail inside, down to the exact position of their table by the window.

Yet, the evening passed without any earth-shattering occurrences. If anything, the two proceeded slowly along the road to true love. No written rules, no conventional strategies. Their approach to one another was cautious, like airplanes maneuvering on the approach to a difficult landing strip.

A mere sexual episode is intensely lived and consummated quickly.

Genuine love is built through hard work and controlled enthusiasm over time.

They began seeing each other once a week, then twice, and then more often. In between times, they spoke a lot on the telephone and during long walks in Central Park, shared their dreams with one another.

One Saturday morning Brian invited Barbara to play tennis at his club. That afternoon there wasn't much to do on the Jersey side of the George Washington Bridge, so they went to Brian's apartment for a drink and to listen to records. The music, the brandy, the talk, and long looks into each other's eyes led

to caresses, cheeks brushing up against one another…in short, love-passion won out.

Brian had not had much experience sexually, but that afternoon it seemed to him that, lying in bed with Barbara on the third floor of the apartment building, the ceiling of the room disappeared, exposing a view of the open sky. It was an intensely colored firmament, new to the eyes of a man who until then had never experienced the reality of love-passion. The extraordinary thing was that Barbara experienced the same overwhelming feeling in her own way.

Love may be a blessing from above, but it may also be a "storm warning" that heralds disaster and tragedy. Without realizing it, the two had put themselves into a volatile situation.

All of these sensations, however, remained locked up inside them, just barely touching the surface among endearments, intimate glances, caresses, adoring smiles and passionate kisses.

In truth, it was Brian who was unable to abandon himself completely. A sense of respect for what he truly loved and cared about restrained him, kept him from indulging in more intimate sexual games. Barbara perceived Brian's difficulty. So as not to upset the tenderness of the moment, she prudently held herself in check, too. This, however, proved somewhat daunting, because she had always abandoned herself fully to desire, rejecting the laws of respectability, so deeply embedded by hypocritical religion.

While she agreed that it was right not to get carried away and pursue passion to excess, she felt that it was absurd to see "sin" in every sensual aspect of life, to fetter human beings' natural urges, and thus make them easy prey to overindulgence once the dam holding back their passions crumbled. Unfortunately, such puritanical attitudes were widespread in the United States.

Barbara had traveled a great deal and noted that in those countries where young people are not prohibited from drinking, the problem of alcoholism was less common. Not allowing people to legally imbibe so much as a can of beer until the age of 21 almost guaranteed, like a time bomb, an explosive overreaction at some point. And the same went for sex.

Too much regulation not only led to excess, but often to uncontrollable degeneration. It was not really healthy to suffocate a physical need which is such a basic element of life. It was better to learn how to use it wisely and channel it.

Barbara could see that something of this sort was oppressing Brian. It was this understanding that made her realize that she loved him all the more. She felt great tenderness for him, such a pleasant, skillful, sweet and sensitive man, who was also a bit mixed up. Surely Brian's sensitivity had made it harder on him, leading him to recognize the bonds created by society, and make them his own without asking himself questions or rebelling.

Barbara saw what a deliberate, self-constructed man Brian was.

He had built his character by placing one brick on top of another in order to shape the structure of his own existence, and he thought more about responsibility than pleasure. But Barbara also appreciated these qualities in him, which today have generally fallen by the wayside in a world where whining and complaining abounds, summed up and excused by the word "stress."

And so Barbara's initial disappointment turned to respect and admiration. She knew that for their relationship to grow, it was imperative to leaf very slowly through their book of love.

That night, after they had made love, they slept separately—Barbara in the bedroom, Brian on the couch in the living room—as if by mutual understanding; and this was a positive and pleasant experience for both of them.

Over the next year, Barbara engaged in much delicate work to succeed in teaching Brian's body to vibrate with passion, and for his soul to accept his heart's plea to yield to the pleasure of love.

To reach the "happy ending," if that's what we may call it, it took 14 months.

One fine sunny morning they were married in a church near the home of Brian's parents, with Barbara's family attending from Chicago. Following the ceremony and reception at their favorite club, they left for the airport to begin their honeymoon.

They had decided on Chile—with its Andes and the Pacific Ocean. It was a perfect choice, since Brian loved the mountains, while Barbara was more inclined towards the sea.

When the hatch of the plane closed, both felt that the rest of the world was now far, far away. Relaxing in his comfortable business class seat, Brian felt all his worries over "building his life" dissipate, and in their wake, he left behind his painstaking stacking of bricks in order to build what now became their life.

This sudden abandonment was a new experience for him, and he owed so much to Barbara, who had sparked in him an entirely new view of life—build your future, but take time out to nourish your spirit with what may seem like useless and non-utilitarian things, but which are necessary for a complete, fulfilling life.

For her part, Barbara was happy, like someone who had succeeded in crossing a beautiful but hard-won mountain range, and had at last reached a hospitable green valley, to find her home and walk through the door into her own little realm.

Perceiving the fulfillment of Brian's soul and knowing that she herself had inspired in him an openness to life and living, she felt gratified and devoted to her "new" man who was no longer afraid to daydream.

Fifteen days later they returned to New Jersey to a beautiful townhouse that they had bought before their wedding near a park.

Brian went back to work, and Barbara got busy making their new place a home. She treated it as a thrilling and pleasurable game, a prize she had won for all that she had succeeded in creating in the encounter of two souls.

Brian was well aware of the importance that Barbara had assumed in his life, and he was very grateful to her. At work he put his nose to the grindstone to be able to add more bricks to the building of their future, and have more free time to spend together to play.

They took short trips nearly every weekend, and although Brian was still the same serious, productive and good man as before, there now shone a new light in his eyes.

The two talked of having children, but Barbara managed, with a struggle, to convince Brian to wait.

She said, "Let's get organized. I know that you've had it drummed into you that marriage was founded to form families with children, but there are also other important aspects of the union between two people. Let's experience them all!"

Ever so slowly, Brian began to share her views.

Being a highly active woman, Barbara began to look for a new occupation, which would give her a creative outlet.

She found a job in an advertising agency. The work was engaging and demanding. A few evenings a week, she would get home after Brian.

This was not to his liking. He thought it was wrong that she should work such long hours. He was the one who should be working harder. This was an old-fashioned concept of male and female roles, but it had been inculcated into him since he was a child, and it was something he couldn't overcome. The situation led to frequent arguments between them.

When Brian complained to his friends, some of them started to say behind his back that he was jealous and that Barbara, so full of life, had begun to grow tired of him. To his face, however, they insisted that things would turn out all right.

And so Brian and Barbara's life together continued with the ups and downs typical of a couple in love, especially when both have strong-willed personalities and their points of view differ on some subjects. To be sure, this became something positive in their relationship. It made their lives more interesting and gave them both a chance to learn and gain from new experiences. Whatever disagreements they may have had, they found ways to resolve them, and the fundamental bond between them remained strong.

When he got to this point in the story, Padre Brian's face changed expression and became suddenly very tense. Gone was that sense of serenity that had descended on him up to that moment. He seemed to be reawakening from a bad dream.

He checked the time on his watch and said, "It is late. I must go to bed. I will continue another day with this story. Please forgive me."

He didn't give them time or any excuses to try to stop him. He waved his hand goodbye and in a few seconds he was out the door.

Sara and Albert rose from their chairs, startled by the change in their friend, but they respected him too much to question his sudden desire for privacy.

Sara was the first to break the silence. "What was that all about? A dream or a reality? A confession or a message? Perhaps a message for us."

Albert's retort conveyed his discontent. "I believe," he said, "that this damn Jesuit is once again trying to play some tricks on us in order to steer our relationship where he wants it to go."

Sara turned on him with vehemence. "Stop, Albert! Sometimes you are too negative. We already agreed that he is a very good man who loves to help people. Instead of reacting like a typical macho man, try to ask your soul—which, as you know, is quite gentle—what this is really all about.

It is very difficult to hide anything from this man, and I believe he saw that there are hidden places in our happy-go-lucky relationship that we never had the courage to talk or even think about. But he is not the issue!"

"Why are you saying this?" Albert's voice was barely a whisper.

"Come on, Albert. Don't try to play the role of the castaway with me. Admit that something has happened in your life that you are not willing to share with me."

Albert stared at the floor, his jaw clenched.

"What am I to you?" she challenged him.

He remained silent. The side of his character that combined stubbornness and insecurity was getting the upper hand. But he could not deny the intense emotion in Sara's words.

When he looked up, he could see in her eyes a kind of violent expression, a powerful light shining, and he realized that something unexpected, something momentous, was about to happen.

They were standing in the middle of the living room when Sara moved close to him, as if she were gathering all her strength to face a life or death decision. When she spoke, her voice had a quality he had not heard before.

The Castaway

20

The next day nothing important happened. Sara and Albert woke up late and didn't talk about the events of the night before. They exchanged some vague pleasantries over breakfast and, since they were both very curious about Padre Brian's story, they agreed that they had to find a way to press him to continue it.

Just before noon someone knocked at the door. It was a young woman who worked at the kindergarten. She asked if they could come to a party in honor of Sara in five days' time.

They were surprised and agreed right away.

After the door closed behind their visitor, Albert was amazed at the joy that radiated from Sara. Indeed, she started to jump up and down like a teenager who has just been asked to the prom.

Before he knew it she ended up in his arms, and they gave each other a number of kisses.

"How different she is from yesterday evening," Albert thought, and felt for the first time proud of her and happy to be in tune with her once again.

Over the next few days they behaved like tourists, driving around, visiting the Mayan ruins in the area, taking pictures, stopping in restaurants for food and refreshment, and buying some small trinkets to keep as mementos.

Several times they talked on the phone with Padre Brian, but he claimed to be very busy, and they had the feeling that he was not in the mood to talk.

The party at the kindergarten turned out to be a big event.

It was a beautiful day, and when Sara and Albert drove up to the gate in their car, they had some difficulty in recognizing the building that should've been so familiar to them.

Outside the fence there were cars parked everywhere. Inside the compound they saw a forest of brightly colored umbrellas bearing logos of different soft drinks, ice cream and other food products. Presumably, they had been borrowed from the local bars and sidewalk cafes to protect the tables scattered around the playground from the burning sun. White sheets were hanging from the front of the building and being held up by an intricate system of wooden poles that kept them taut, creating a large canopy, a kind of temporary porch, where tables filled with food and beverages beckoned. There was also a large table that seemed to be intended for important guests.

The whole compound looked like a frenetic colony of ants, but without any purposeful organization. Children were running around excitedly, and teachers tried their best to contain them. Some adults were helping themselves to the food at the tables, while others were talking in small groups, as if waiting for the real festivities to begin.

As Albert and Sara emerged from their car, the scene changed instantly, and it became clear that everyone had been waiting for their arrival. The children assembled in various groups around the yard as if on cue and started to sing in very loud voices in a somewhat confused fashion. But the name "Sara" could be heard clearly many times.

By the time the guests of honor had entered the gate, the adults all raised their glasses and cheered. They surrounded them with smiles and called out their names.

Then all the children descended on them jumping, talking, nattering and screaming like a happy army of fans crowding around a pair of movie stars stepping from a limousine onto the red carpet.

Sara stood in their midst petrified. Tears came to her eyes and she was incapable of speech.

The new kindergarten director, Padre Brian and the mayor came up to her and shook her hand, and all the children erupted in another riot of excitement. It took a long time to restore some semblance of order.

On their way to the table under the canopy, Sara and Albert had to shake many hands—teachers, aides, parents, and important figures of the community. They were guided to take their places at the center of the table. Soon they were treated to a number of short speeches that expressed enthusiasm and gratitude toward Sara for her service to the children, and pleasure and good wishes for the castaway and his fairy tale ending.

Padre Brian didn't say anything. In his unassuming and effective way, he was making sure that everything ran smoothly, but his eyes shone with a special joy whenever he glanced toward her. They seemed to say: "Here is my tribute to you, my very dear Sara, and to your man."

The lunch that was served consisted of a great variety of potluck dishes that had been made by parents, friends and the kindergarten staff. Everyone ate their fill. At various times, different guests got up and offered toasts, and the teachers tried to keep the children entertained with games and little prizes.

It was a happy, carnival-like atmosphere. But at a certain point, Padre Brian decided it was time to conclude the event while everything was in high spirits. He got up and thanked everyone. He invited the guests to take home with them the aura of happiness that surrounded them at that moment, as well as any leftover food.

There was more chatting and chattering, and goodbyes and kisses for Sara and Albert, as people reluctantly gathered their belongings and headed for their cars.

Sara and Albert were among the last to leave. Heading down the dirt road, they looked back and waved in response to the loud farewells of the children who surrounded Padre Brian at the gate.

His look was radiant, but also filled with melancholy.

Albert drove and Sara looked back several more times until, after a few bends in the road, she could no longer see the kindergarten. They were sated and had the feeling that they were leaving behind an important period of their lives. As this chapter closed, they had the sense that they were coming up on the crest of a mountain, ready to face the rest of fhe world from high above.

Yes, on the verge, but not yet completely ready. There were still things to be cleared up before they could proceed unencumbered and cut all their ties to the past.

The Castaway

21

For the next two days, Sara and Albert visited many of their friends and acquaintances, thanking them. They enjoyed going around the town, experiencing their moment of fame and basking in the happiness and gratitude the community was eager to bestow on them.

Padre Brian called only once to compliment Sara and Albert for the way they had handled themselves at the party and to mention that he was going away for two days. He would call again when he returned.

It was strange, both because he left the area so suddenly, and because he seemed to have chosen such an odd time to disappear.

But Padre Brian was Padre Brian—a protagonist that always came back to reclaim his chosen part.

In his absence, Albert and Saran took the opportunity to visit the nearby Mayan ruins, something they hadn't done in all their time in the Yucatan. They also thought a great deal about the story he had begun to tell them. They tried to understand what it meant and why he had told it to them. But, for some reason, they did so separately, both deciding to keep their thoughts to themselves.

It was too early to discuss it with one another, especially since it was still in the making, and they feared they might reach the wrong conclusion, not just for Padre Brian's sake, but for their own as well.

They were becoming wiser without realizing it.

Four days later Padre Brian called and invited Sara and Albert to his house for dinner the next evening.

When they arrived, Padre Brian could read in their bearing the growing effects of his efforts on their behalf, and it gave him a moment of considerable pleasure.

It was a night like many others they had spent together. After they had their fill of eating, drinking and talking about the party, and commenting on the happy atmosphere and the many different people they had met, Sara used a lull in conversation to ask Padre Brian if he would please go on with his story. She told him they had spent much of their days thinking about him and would really love to know more of it, in no small part because it could be helpful to them.

That was exactly what the Jesuit had been waiting for.

He moved over into the big armchair with a glass of water in his hand. For a few moments he seemed lost and uncomfortable, trying to find his train of thought, going from the present moment to a past that, judging from the change in his expression, was quite painful. But like a good actor, he soon grew into the role he had chosen and picked up the narrative where he'd left off.

For three years he and Barbara lived a normal life of husband and wife. There were good times and periods of conflict, as in all marriages. Overall, they grew closer and more accepting in their relationship of each other's differences.

One night, though, Barbara never made it home.

At first Brian thought that she was working very late again, but then he got concerned. He called her on her office phone but she didn't answer. As the hours went by, Brian called a few of Barbara's co-workers, but none of them knew anything specific.

All that Brian could find out was that she had left the office around 6:30 p.m. Now it was three and a half hours later. Something was very wrong.

Brian had never felt so tense, yet feeble when it came to making a decision. Should he look for her in the neighborhood? Or call the police and the hospitals to see if there had been an accident?

He did contact various acquaintances. Speaking to one of them in particular, he could hear that the voice on the other end of the line sounded somewhat off-key. Perhaps he was being a nuisance.

Stuck in the apartment, he felt helpless and wracked with anxiety. He moved from one chair to the next, turned the television on and off repeatedly, went to the kitchen, threw himself onto the bed.

What could he do?

He felt out of his depth—he who had always been the one to find a practical solution in every situation. He who was known for his common sense and his decision-making ability felt completely at a loss.

He considered filing a missing persons report with the police, though Barbara wasn't the type to just disappear on her own. He went to the telephone several times, picked up the receiver, but then decided to wait a little while longer. He knew that they wouldn't take him seriously for the first 24 hours anyway.

Exhausted and completely bewildered, he drifted off into a fitful sleep on the couch.

It was 4 a.m. when he woke with a start. Perhaps Barbara had come back quietly, not wanting to wake him.

Frantically he looked through the entire house, but she was not there. Now he was desperate. He decided it was time to call the police. He picked up the phone and forced himself to clearly explain the situation.

An hour or so later, a detective showed up at his door with his partner walking up behind him.

For the first time in his life Brian was in a state of semi-derangement. He felt utterly lost. The two detectives asked him a slew of questions which he found useless, almost idiotic.

He thought, "This is the typical routine of men who work for the government, wasting taxpayers' money instead of making quick decisions and taking immediate action."

He wanted to yell at them, "Do something!"

But they left politely, muttering platitudes that were meant to reassure, but had the opposite effect. Brian could not get a grip on what was happening, he knew only that the wheels of bureaucracy or justice had begun to move their sluggish gears.

In the morning, a friend came to his aid. He called Brian's office with an excuse for his absence. He also contacted his doctor, who provided sedatives.

At last Brian slipped into a deep sleep, the sleep of oblivion and unconsciousness that allows humanity to regain strength and persevere.

Padre Brian paused and looked up at his guests like a lost, sad child.

Albert, his eyes wide with dismay, mirrored his distress and was incapable of uttering a word.

Sara came to their rescue and said, "It is a miracle, a testament to the human condition that people find in moments of disaster and extreme difficulty the strength and courage to struggle on with their lives."

Both Padre Brian and Albert nodded, and their features relaxed as one.

The Castaway

22

Being a consummate storyteller, when Padre Brian resumed his narrative, he made Sara and Albert relive his most intense moments, his doubts, his hopes, his illusions and utter dismay when he could not understand where Barbara had gone. For days he could not come to grips with what had happened, not knowing into which void of existence she had disappeared. More than once, he thought he would go mad.

Then events began to snowball, moving faster than he'd ever before known. The newspapers and TV stations picked up on the story, and reporters gathered in front of the house where he lived. The police held press conferences, filled with nothing of substance, but plenty of innuendo.

He hated being in his office, but he forced himself to go. The looks of his co-workers and the phone calls from the police, with their insinuating questions, agitated him.

There were also comments from friends and acquaintances, not stated out loud to his face, but going from mouth to ear and from ear to mouth, and then passed on to another ear behind his back. As a result, Brian was the last one to find out, and when he did, he felt especially hurt.

So he sought shelter at home. But sitting there with nothing to do but brood, he felt like he was losing his mind. So then it was back to the office…to do what?

He did not know.

Brian's parents moved into a hotel near his house to offer him moral support. They saw one another at mealtimes, forcing themselves to create a veneer of normalcy, but few meaningful words were exchanged.

It became clear to Brian that he was being held responsible for the disappearance of his wife. Soon, public opinion, fed by rivers of nonsense that streamed daily from the newspapers and television, turned against him. Everyone assumed he'd had something to do with it.

Wasn't it true that she'd been staying at the office late, and had been neglecting her home life?

What was the reason for that?

Had he been mistreating her?

Was he jealous?

Or worse yet, what dark secrets was he hiding?

Had she found out something she wasn't supposed to know?

Brian began seeing these questions written on the faces of the cops, his co-workers, and even his friends. He did not wish to lend too much importance to them—otherwise it wouldn't have been long before he actually started to feel guilty himself.

Guilty of what? Of loving a woman more than he loved himself? Perhaps he had not known how to satisfy her completely—but was this something for which he should be held accountable?

God knows how hard he had tried to make her happy.

Why, then, did this unspoken accusation upset him so?

When he heard words like, "She'll be back," meant to give comfort, a voice inside him said, "You're never going to see her again."

Then he became upset all over again at the depth of his despair and pessimism.

Had he turned masochistic? Perhaps he had always been and hadn't realized it? He couldn't help but succumb to the exhaustion and his cowardly admission to himself that Barbara was gone forever.

But then, a deeper voice answered. "That's it, I've got to stop thinking about it, I've got to escape this torment. It's best just to admit that she's gone, rather than stoke useless hopes.

I'd do better just to get back to work and act as if nothing had happened.

Just get back to the old routine."

Then the news came like lightning flashing through a tired, gray sky. Barbara had been found—or rather, Barbara's semi-decomposed body had been found. It had been buried in the park she often used to walk through as a shortcut on her way home from the office.

Brian did not have time to completely understand what had happened, as he found himself immersed in a high-profile murder case, the sort that plays out on TV and for which we would not even remotely consider being extras, let alone occupying the starring role.

But Brian became the main character, the prime suspect in the drama—albeit a somewhat awkward, confused, tired one—with all clues pointing in his direction.

He acted like a not very credible character to whom the police gave little credit and even less understanding. It was a nightmarish period in his life.

Tried and convicted in the news media long before the trial, he was in for the fight of his life.

Poor man. What a catastrophe! Albert and Sara were dumbfounded and didn't dare say anything, although they began to entertain certain doubts about their friend. Was that why he had become a priest? To atone for his sins?

Though Padre Brian's involvement in the murder seemed impossible to them, considering his openness and kindness, they harbored a morsel of doubt. It was only natural to wonder whether he had acquired these characteristics in the wake of that awful experience.

Padre Brian guessed what they were thinking, and decided to play along with the ambiguity. This provided him with a modicum of gratification, which was perhaps a bit underhanded and not in line with his calling.

But the man in Padre Brian approved, even if the priest did not, and the Jesuit sided with the man.

Thus, he delved into the details of the police investigation, and the defense strategy for the trial that was to follow. He spent a good deal of time talking about his relationship with his lawyer, who was confident in a positive outcome since evidence against him was at best circumstantial, and rather dubious at that. It bothered Brian, though, that his lawyer never showed any signs of believing in his innocence.

During the ordeal Brian quit his job, sold his house and moved into his parents' home. But he didn't fight the charges, since he could not understand the persistence of his accusers and their desire to destroy even the memory of the only real and truly great love story of his life.

If his mom and dad hadn't been there for him, he would surely have gone mad. There were moments when he had thoughts of killing himself, even though such an act was against his principles as a "man of good sense."

Then, one day, as if an evil spell was suddenly lifted, it was all over—at least for the others.

Two detectives paid him a visit.

They were polite and seemed almost too kind, which led him to imagine that some new disaster was about to strike. But then the older of the two began talking to him in a composed, almost formal manner.

Brian understood only one thing from the entire speech—that they had found the man who had killed Barbara.

The perpetrator had already served time for sex crimes and was a suspect in another murder case the police were working on. Following this trail, they had uncovered conclusive evidence that he was responsible for killing both victims, including Brian's wife. They came off as sorry and regretful, and kept apologizing, yet Brian noticed an undercurrent of satisfaction in their demeanor, as if to say, "We've solved two cases in one fell swoop."

But what about him?

Padre Brian looked up at his guests with a certain sense of irony. He could see a veil of shame as they averted their eyes to avoid his penetrating gaze. It may have been only the sin of presumption that made him feel somehow gratified. In any case, there was also a sense of personal satisfaction that Padre Brian's "image" was safe. He had only been a victim after all.

A long silence followed.

Padre Brian rose, poured himself another glass of water and motioned to his guests, offering them a drink as well.

Albert and Sara shook their heads almost imperceptibly.

It seemed as if they were in a kind of trance, spellbound by Padre Brian's revelations and unable to formulate a response.

"I'm tired," said the Jesuit, who had regained control over himself. "Let's continue another time—tomorrow, if you like."

Grateful, Sara blurted out, "Of course, whenever you want. But you must do it. We would be upset if you didn't finish telling us your life story and all the trials and tribulations you've been through."

Padre Brian nodded in acknowledgment.

He looked at Albert, who remained sitting in his chair as if petrified. At a nudge from Sara, he got up, nodded to the priest without meeting his eyes, and headed outside.

Sara shrugged her shoulders, as if apologizing for him, gave Padre Brian a quick smile and said, "Till tomorrow then."

The Castaway

23

But they did not speak about this matter the next day, nor the day after that. Once again, Padre Brian was very busy. Either that or he wanted to give Albert and Sara some time to process all the ripples and ramifications of the story he'd told as they reflected on their lives. Though they ran into each other again two days later, when Sara asked Padre Brian about getting together in the evening, he begged off with the excuse that he had prior commitments.

Sara and Albert were puzzled when the good Jesuit avoided them. This was not typical behavior from a man who seemed always ready to confront matters head-on.

The strenuousness of his schedule, however, whether genuine or not, did have its desired effect. In discussing the possible reasons for his behavior, Sara and Albert talked of all that they had learned, and their longing to learn more about Brian the young man, Brian the manager, Brian the husband, and Brian the priest and Jesuit.

For Albert, these conversations led to the most important question: How had he turned his life around and reached the decision to become a Jesuit?

Padre Brian had chosen a rather demanding religious order that required culture, dedication and endless study. The Society of Jesus was not a religious order that took in desperate and confused individuals. On the contrary, it attracted academicians and thinkers with well-defined opinions, willing to put them to work, with a precise commitment and within a precise framework.

If Brian the man, after what happened with Barbara, had become so confused and inefficient as he claimed to be in his story, then how had he gone about finding the rationality and the fortitude to take such an important step as entering the Jesuit Order?

The Franciscans might have been more plausible, since they repudiated most of what the world has to offer; or the Dominicans, whose search for extreme spirituality is ongoing. It was hard to guess why he had become a Jesuit.

For all Albert knew, Jesuits were not as service-oriented as Padre Brian. They were more about education, bringing new ideas to life and building bridges between different civilizations and customs. Indeed, Padre Brian was doing what Brian the manager once did, only now in a more in-depth, globalized way, and with the blessing of God.

For Albert, the question boiled down to what had Brian done to heal his wounds not only to go on with his life, but to find meaning in day-to-day existence. Somehow he had found a new arena where he could put to work the skills he had acquired in his previous life, even if they now served a different purpose.

Sara patiently listened to Albert's ruminations with kind encouragement. She had less difficulty accepting Brian's choice, although she, too, was curious as to how it had come about.

They started to meet again more regularly.

Padre Brian looked more relaxed now that he had liberated himself from the weight he had carried for so long. But he was clearly evasive in response to any question regarding his decision to become a Jesuit.

He'd say, "One day I will explain it to you, but allow me for now to just enjoy your company."

Sara nodded her agreement, and Albert did, too, even if he didn't show a great deal of enthusiasm. He wanted to know more and right away, to find a parallel between the priest's and his own life, and to understand the situation in which he and Padre Brian found themselves.

At the same time, the figure of Padre Brian changed in Sara's and Albert's eyes. They each had their separate opinion. They had discussed the matter with each other, but they had kept their examination somewhat superficial in order to protect their relationship and guard their friendship with Padre Brian, whom they now esteemed more than before based on the story he had told them.

The two shared great respect for the Jesuit, a sense of respect that had grown from what they had learned about him. It may have been dictated by compassion for what they had found out about his prior life, or by a sense of guilt over having always used him as a remedy for their problems—while being oblivious to the fact that he had his own cross to bear.

A cavalier attitude is common enough regarding priests, who in a certain sense are considered superior beings until people get to know the details of their lives.

Some of them may very well be superior, since they have willingly chosen that difficult role for themselves. The same, of course, can be said about certain businessmen, engineers, astronauts, doctors and so on.

In any case, Albert and Sara's new understanding would have a profound influence on their relationship with the priest, as would become clear to them shortly after they started to once again meet up regularly and feel closer as a threesome than ever before.

The impact on Albert and Padre Brian, however, was another matter entirely. The two men shared a special familiar feeling which made them act differently toward one another than they had in the past. And what did the two men see now, behind the appearance of this exotic kindergarten principal? What were their feelings about her?

Now that they had let a few too many words slip, what emotion was inspired in them by Sara's gifts of goodness, beauty, intelligence and sexuality?

Albert often found himself a spectator, watching the special way Padre Brian used to address Sara—a mix of fatherly protection, profound friendship, and uncommon respect with a touch of familiarity that bordered on something more intimate. At any rate, the admiration was genuine—a kind of platonic love, which at times might appear to verge on real love with all its desires.

In the past, Albert had experienced this perception as a fleeting intuition, something he considered a figment of his imagination. But

now he was no longer sure that it was his mind playing tricks on him. Still, deep down, what did it matter?

Marianne had taught him how useless jealousy was.

It was true…perhaps Padre Brian was suffering, and Sara felt this—and the difficulties created other problems among them, even if it were only a spiritual matter.

As Albert contemplated this issue, pacing in the living room of his house, he exclaimed, "Only spiritually! Why do I say 'only'?" and continued more quietly, "as if it were of little importance and represented a limitation of a feeling of love?"

Actually, it's the opposite that occurs.

He knew how sexual desire takes hold with violence, then slowly relents; although it may return in mercurial spurts, at first closer together, then farther apart, the ebb and flow like waves at sea when the stormy wind dies down. Spiritual involvement, on the other hand, is solid and lasting. But if it cannot be put in perspective with the values of life, it can lead to debasement and dangerous delusions.

He repeated out loud, "Only spirituality—it doesn't make sense!"

Sara heard him from the next room—the door was ajar —and was amazed. She worried that he was becoming too obsessive again.

She let several minutes pass, then went to Albert and said, "Let's take a ride in the car. I want to really imprint these places and these people upon my memory. I have the feeling we're not going to be here much longer, and I so want to cherish all I've learned here in the Yucatan and from Padre Brian. I think it would be difficult, if not impossible, to imagine all this in New York or in any other city in the United States."

Albert was driving along the main street heading out of town when Sara turned toward him with kindness and asked, "What do you think the future has in store for us? I've always hesitated to ask you this question because I didn't want to break the spell we've been under.

It's as if we were suspended between our past lives, laden with disquieting memories, and the pleasure of living in the present and exploring ourselves and the world with new eyes."

She paused for a moment, placed a hand on his thigh, and continued.

"But we can't always go on like this. All roads lead somewhere, and when you come to a fork in the road, you've got to make a decision…I'm a little frightened by this. It must have been hearing Padre Brian's story, which really touched me, especially the cruelty of his loss.

But…there's more to it than that. You've experienced something similar, you can relate to it, and I can see that it disturbs you.

So where do I fit into all of this in relation to you?

I've even noticed a hint of jealousy in your words to Padre Brian, a tension between you two that I had never imagined would be there.

Go ahead, tell me I'm naïve, I won't take offense.

On the contrary, I feel as though I've woken up and have begun to look around—and what I think I see, or feel, frightens me."

"What are you talking about?!" interrupted Albert.

He tried to conceal his embarrassment, as it suddenly became clear to him that Sara was well aware of his doubts in regard to her relationship with Padre Brian.

He stammered, "Don't ruin all we have by trying to make plans and looking for explanations to clear up…to clear up what?

Just what is there to clear up between us? We like being together, we've got lots in common, we complement one another.

What more do you want? For me that's already a lot.

Without you, I'd go back to being Joe..."

He stopped short, confused, as if he'd revealed more than he had wanted.

The silence between them grew tense, like the charged atmosphere before a storm. The ghosts of Joe, Marianne, Padre Brian, and his friends in Florida were taking shape in his mind.

All his ghosts!

He realized, perhaps for the first time, that his relationship with Sara at this point was the only thing that was real, new and promising in his life. And yet, how selfish he had been, and how he had taken advantage of her help and support without taking any interest in her past and experiences.

Who knows whether Padre Brian had guessed as much and had comforted and helped Sara or whether he, like Albert, had made use of her beauty, goodness and kindness just to heal his own wounds?

He found a bit of solace in the possibility that perhaps the Jesuit might share in his guilt. Then he dismissed the comparison from his mind. Attributing similar selfishness to the priest in order to justify his own seemed the height of pettiness indeed.

He pulled the car over to the side of the road. He knew he had to talk to Sara, to reach her somehow. He put his hands to her face.

Then he said, "Forgive me. Sometimes I feel as though I live off your every breath. I catch myself looking at you in awe, as if you were some kind of goddess detached from my own mortal existence and ultimately inaccessible.

Please, help me cross this rift that still appears to separate us.
Actually, you have never fully opened yourself to me.

Do it, I beg of you.

I think it will give me the power to map out a future for us
together. And that's something which, in reality, I've never, ever
been able to contemplate doing by myself."

Sara took his hands in her own and gave him a quick kiss.
Then she placed them back on the steering wheel.

"Drive us home, you nitwit! It's all not as hard as you think,
and you don't have to reprimand yourself for anything.

We'll come up with a plan together, and it won't be long before we realize it. I think I love you, in a spiritual sense as well."

For a moment, Albert looked at her with almost fearful intensity. The word "spiritual" was truly becoming a nightmare.
All he wanted to do was live, live sincerely and enjoy the simple
things of this world. And perhaps there was a chance...she personified the chance...

A miniscule smile tugged at the corners of his mouth. He
started up the motor and drove back home.

The Castaway

24

Clouds seemed to gather and suddenly pull apart in layers as if trying to escape the incoming wind. At intervals, rain seemed to cover the entire scene like a billowing curtain – a thick, noisy, solid curtain that crashed down on trees, streets and homes, only to liquefy and transform into sinuous water that penetrated furrows and filled the meager spaces of ground between one building and another. It was a gift from the tropical depression that hovered offshore in the Gulf.

In the tropics, even average rainstorms are powerful enough to appear unreal and overwhelming, though usually they are brief.

A station wagon pulled up in front of Albert and Sara's house. Padre Brian, wearing a big raincoat with a hood, dashed out of the vehicle and took refuge on the front porch. He knocked and at the same time grabbed the handle of the door, which suddenly flew open; he was driven inside by the wind as if the fury of the elements had justified him bursting into his friends' home.

Albert looked up, hardly realizing what was going on. He was lying on the couch, his head on Sara's lap, and wearing only a pair of workout shorts. With one hand Sara was caressing his hair, while her other hand was lost inside his shorts.

Sara remained there, immobile. She made no effort to pull back her hand or compose herself, but looked at the priest dispassionately.

This was their home, and the storm was outside. How could they have expected Padre Brian to bring the storm with him, into their living room?

"The door was open," Padre Brian stammered. "I put my hand on the doorknob simply for support in order to knock, and all of a sudden I wound up inside, as if the wind had pushed me.

I apologize, I see that I'm disturbing you. I'll leave at once."

He shook off his embarrassment and was about to turn on his heels to head back toward the front door, when Albert stopped him.

He sat up with a start and said, "Don't go!

Stay with us! We were just a bit mesmerized by the storm, watching it from the window that faces west. Your entrance made us think a tornado had blown in. But it was only you, you old devil of a Jesuit, so fond of scaring the wits out of poor sinners like us."

They all laughed at that, and the atmosphere seemed to return to normal, although something remained in the air even after Albert had put on his polo shirt and Sara had straightened her skirt, which had revealed something more than just a glimpse of her thighs.

The moment of intimacy he had so brusquely interrupted brought a flood of memories to Brian's mind of his happy times with Barbara. Over the years he had learned to put such memories aside, to shut them away in a remote area of his brain. But more recently, as if by some strange alchemy, they had become unlocked, and he had begun to revisit them with relative ease.

He considered that the initial cause might have been all those long hours spent working with Sara. It had all taken place with unaffected naturalness, nothing unwholesome about it. On the contrary, it had reawakened a sweetness in him that had been lying dormant all his life and which he never knew he possessed.

It looked like everything had gone back to normal. They all lounged in the living room, each with a glass of fruit juice in hand. Albert and Sara sat on the couch, and Padre Brian occupied a comfortable armchair on the other side of the coffee table. Padre Brian started to describe a moment at the party that had given him a clear understanding of how much Albert and Sara were in love.

He had experienced much pleasure at the time.

But as he tried to explain his feeling to them about how beautiful and highly esteemed Sara had been, he could not get out of his mind the scene of intimacy he had just interrupted a few minutes earlier.

And suddenly, Padre Brian felt overwhelmed by his own memories, which he had put carefully aside for so long.

Those strong, repressed feelings had come to the surface, like a river overflowing its levees. Their vehemence and urgency took him by surprise and plunged him into a tortuous, intricate monologue whose twists and turns became rather difficult for Sara and Albert to follow.

Sara, who understood the awkward situation in which Padre Brian had put himself, insisted that he continue his history. He owed that to them.

It took him some time to recover his equilibrium and, with an expression of gratitude, resume his narrative.

"The end of that whole storm, or better, hurricane, which struck both my own life and Barbara's, left me in a daze—as if I had been given a heavy dose of sedatives. Nothing mattered. I was unable to react to anything that occurred in my immediate surroundings, let alone to any news of what went on in society at large. My mother, who was very close to me, may have been the only one able to reach my heart once in a while.

When my old friends and colleagues spoke to me, it left me indifferent; their attentions irked me just enough to shake me out of my apathy and find an excuse for leaving their presence.

After a while I realized it wasn't their fault, but I had acquired a strong sense of skepticism toward all of mankind, and I shunned the company of others because I couldn't stomach their hypocrisy.

"Did the latter phase last long?" Sara broke in, her face taut and concerned, and pained over his suffering.

"I got better after two or three years," Padre Brian replied. "Such a serious illness calls for a long convalescence—and to tell the truth, I never completely recovered."

He hesitated, then suddenly got up from his chair and took one step toward the window. A shiver seemed to run across his shoulders and he straightened his bent frame. When he turned back to Albert and Sara, his eyes radiated with passion.

"At this point, I have a confession to make to you, Sara. You are the only person who, as if by magic, has been able to wipe away the fog that has engulfed my spirit, even if just for a short time."

The tension in the room became palpable.

Padre Brian was amazed that he had succeeded to express himself so openly.

Sara, ever sensitive to Albert's feelings, tried to forestall any angry reaction from him. Smiling, she lightly caressed his arm.

Albert, for his part, was equally amazed that he felt no animosity or jealousy toward the priest, only a sense of compassion. He did feel scrutinized by the others, so he nodded as if to say, "I already knew it."

Then, he turned to Padre Brian. "Finally you lift the weight from your soul. I, too, traveled the same road.

How strange, that the same woman would help both of us, though in different ways, to understand life."

The look of surprise on Sara's face yielded to complacency, the kind of contented glow women have once they've finally gotten proof of what they have known intuitively for a long time.

She rose slowly, took Padre Brian's hands in hers, lifted them to her cheeks, and said, "I'm touched, or should I say, honored that I've had such an impact on your life.

But what do you mean when you say that I 'wiped away the fog…just for a short time'?

I feel as though I've added insult to injury instead of giving you comfort."

"No, no, rest easy," said the Jesuit, softly, "you've provided me with enormous relief, more than you'll ever imagine! Even the appearance of Albert was a big help to me. It made me realize that I was an old priest carrying a great burden that even my well-defined mission—which had become fundamental for me—couldn't lighten.

Let me be clear. I never once had any doubts about the choice I'd made. But it exacted a considerable toll and was often more difficult than I could bear."

"How did you make that choice?" asked Sara, gently.

"With the help of an elderly Jesuit I met by chance, just like my meeting Joe—sorry, Albert.

He managed to show me, thanks to the depths of his knowledge and the transparency of his spirituality, a new direction in life, which became the key to my existence."

Albert got up to refill their glasses. An ironic smile played about his lip as he asked, "How did you meet him?"

The tension in the room had subsided, and Padre Brian waited until they had all settled back in their seats and were sipping their drinks before he continued with his story.

"It was a strange coincidence, the way most important things in life happen, actually. I was at a restaurant with my mother. The evening dragged on mercilessly. I was filled with regret over making her life difficult with my apathy, even if she never gave up and kept pushing me to elicit some, any reaction.

At the table next to us sat a tall, thin elderly man with splendid white, well-coifed hair who looked to be about 75, perhaps 80 years old.

What particularly struck me about him was his face—it was still handsome and full of life. His profile was marked by a prominent nose and a longish jaw. His two light-blue eyes expressed kindness and demanded respect. He smiled, observing all that went on around him with interest and curiosity, as if he were a natural part of the surroundings.

That was when it happened. That was the significant moment.

As the evening went on, I noticed the man watching us a few times. It seemed as though his table had become part of ours and that we'd become intimate friends, even though he'd never said a word.

It was just his face, his eyes and occasional nods that seemed to take part in our mundane conversation.

He finished eating before we did. I think he'd been sitting there for some time before we entered. He asked for the check and got ready to leave. Then he pulled from his pocket a slip of paper and a pen, wrote a few lines, and approached our table, saying, as if it were the most normal thing in the world, 'Call me. I'd like very much to invite you to dinner. Believe me, you need to speak to me. I have a lot of things to say that would interest you. At most, you'll be wasting a couple hours. I have a somewhat strange name, I've written it on this note.

I'm a Jesuit priest—but don't worry, in this case, religion has nothing to do with it.'

My mother tried to get up to pay her respects, but he placed a hand on her shoulder and said, 'It is not necessary. Thank you, anyhow. Sometimes people shy away as soon as they hear I'm a priest.'

He handed me the note, bowed graciously, first to my mother, then to me, and said his goodbyes.

All I was able to mumble was, 'My pleasure.'

We watched him leave the restaurant.

We saw that other people were watching him too."

A faraway expression appeared on Padre Brian's face, as if he were seeing the mysterious stranger in his mind's eye.

When he returned to the present, he saw Albert and Sara looking at him like children captivated by a fairy tale.

"Enough," he huffed. "Time for a glass of wine. Long stories are boring. But, if you're interested, the tale will be continued."

Although they both nodded eagerly, the story did not resume that evening.

They dined together, at first with a little embarrassment, then with great pleasure.

The wind had died down. The storm, with its thunder and lightning and pouring rain, had gone elsewhere. Temporary peace had returned.

As they headed outside for an after-dinner walk, they all felt sated and tired from all that had transpired that day. Such revelations, like heavy meals and aged wines, require a little time to be digested.

Now they knew what reality was, and could measure it. That night none of them had the need or strength to ask themselves the meaning of the word "reality" or whether in life, "reality" even existed.

The Castaway

25

Over the next few days, they met a few more times, and Padre Brian filled them in on what had happened after that fateful meeting at the restaurant.

The description of young Brian's rebirth, his initiation into the faith, and most importantly, his newfound vocation for helping those in need, was told quickly, in a handful of brief and simple episodes.

Faith and love for others, including animals and all that surrounds us, are such simple sentiments. So much so that they don't create any waves or make the evening news, thus escaping the attention and interest of the rest of the world.

Padre Brian never mentioned the name of the man he'd met in the restaurant—a man so profound and attuned to the vibrations of others' souls, one who carried with him a tradition of culture, experience, along with a quickness of mind and a vision of life to help people.

"He was better than the majority of psychologists that come out of the colleges and universities today," Padre Brian said, adding, "It is unfortunate that we don't learn at school how to develop the faculties that have been given to us at birth, along with the curiosity to discover and experience, and a sensitivity for understanding others. School helps us only to sharpen our technical skills, sometimes not even related to our talents.

I was very lucky that all these innate qualities of this man's soul were available to help me – and many others he met—to get over my ordeal."

Sara and Albert also learned that this old Jesuit spoke five languages, besides Latin, had lived in many different parts of the world, and had written essays and historical monographs. He came from an old American family of Anglo-Saxon stock, though, thanks to his paternal grandmother, a little Italian blood also ran in his veins.

But the further Padre Brian went on with the story of how he became a Jesuit, even when told over a series of episodes,and the more he expounded on the details, reasons and processes involved, the harder it became for Albert and Sara to take it all in.

Great changes in the human spirit provoke a certain irritation in listeners. The first questions that spontaneously arise are:

"Why not me?"

"Why has this man been shown the way and not me?"

And Albert was not immune from this feeling, so he thought, "Yes, I enjoy the relationship with Sara, and this has helped me a lot, but I don't really have a clue of what I want to do with my life.

Why must I continue to grope through the shadows in search of it?"

The truth is, we shuffle about the shadows continuously. However, if everything were completely dark, we would not even have the incentive to seek a path to follow.

The day was hot, without the slightest breeze – one of those days in which the atmosphere presses with all its weight upon the body. Albert was behind the wheel and Sara was alongside him as they drove to pick up Padre Brian to visit the kindergarten together. Albert suddenly seemed to awaken from the funk into which he had fallen and said aloud, almost shouting, "Enough, enough...enough!"

"Enough what?" Sara asked.

"Enough," he continued. "Enough of all this cogitation, enough of all this continuous doubt about why we're here in this world and what we should be doing with our existence. Enough of these stories that demand such deep commitment."

He hesitated, then went on with a tone of voice that conveyed a sense of discomfort. "I'm tired of hearing the word 'spiritual' repeated over and over again.

Tell me, what's so spiritual about life on planet Earth? Maybe more than we realize, but...I'm convinced that thinking too much about it leads only to confusion."

A moment of deep silence followed, then Sara said with disarming simplicity, "Stop the car. Calm down and touch me. I'll prove to you that we're here now, alive in the flesh."

Albert did as he was told. Sara reached over and enfolded him in her arms. Their deep embrace convinced one another, without a word, that they could leave that uncertainty behind and avoid being lured into a state of doubt and remorse which woukd have led both to near delirium. They had the certainty that they were thinking in unison.

And Albert confirmed, "We've got to get away from the one who breathed life into our love."

They looked into each other's eyes, again without a word. Their decision, though undeclared, was final, and they moved into action quickly.

Theirs was true love. Any further delving into how the two had found one another and what it meant would have been useless, and dangerous.

They smiled, kissed, and went back to the house. From there they phoned Padre Brian to tell him they would not come to pick him up. Then they called the airline and booked a flight to Sarasota.

They planned to stay there for a few days to enjoy the relaxing atmosphere of that city and its beaches, and to let themselves sway to the colors of that special sky—and decide their next move.

The following day they stopped by to see the "good Jesuit" and give him the news. Although they were clear-headed about their decision, they approached him like two schoolchildren taking leave of their professor.

Padre Brian immediately understood what was happening and made it easy for them to depart without an overemotional goodbye.

Enough had already been said. Perhaps neither of them figured it would be a lengthy absence, since together they had laid down roots in the Yucatan and created bonds based on shared experiences that would never be forgotten.

Padre Brian waved to them as they got into their car and drove off. Sara and Albert were leaving for Florida, but they would be back, and he would once again be able to look into Sara's eyes and feel a bit of warmth in his old veins. He'd be able to experience the joy of seeing the two together, their love the fruit of his perspicacity and meticulous work. He would see reflected in them what he had found for an all-too-short time in his own life so many years ago. He would revel in his victory over destiny, which had treated him so cruelly in his youth.

In the meantime, he would take pride in keeping alive all the charitable institutions built and kept running thanks to his contributions. That would be gratifying indeed.

Such were his thoughts as he watched Sara and Albert's car disappear. At last, for a moment, everything appeared wonderful, almost perfect. Almost.

The Castaway

EPILOGUE

Though it was late, Padre Brian was still sitting at his desk, trying to come up with a new project for himself, but he felt drained of his usual enthusiasm. His mind wandered lazily, from one detail to the next, reviewing without any particular logic the recent occurrences and the emotions they stirred.

Among this muddle of thoughts, his mind managed to focus on a curious statistic he'd heard a few days earlier on a television news program: By far, the most widely visited websites are those that feature either sex or religion.

He no longer remembered the exact number of annual visits, but he clearly recalled that the numbers were considerably larger than those racked up by other kinds of websites, and that the sex sites were only slightly ahead of the religious sites.

It occurred to him that he too, in his small way, had benefited from learning from both worlds, though he had never been keen enough to thoroughly understand why they held such fascination for so many people.

How ironic that the business world spent so much energy and money on getting people to visit their websites, whereas for sex and religion, popularity came naturally.

He felt slightly stupid. He had gotten a taste of the world of sex and was deeply involved in the world of religion, but he had somehow underestimated their full potential and possibilities.

The most disconcerting thing was how, after so many years, a simple statistic could induce him to re-examine the values in his life.

It had taken television, with its screen so rich in color and lacking in reality, to make him understand that he had been trapped by the simplistic idea of doing something practical, so that people might communicate, so that they might love, understand and help one another.

How could he have focused his whole life on that and put all the other opportunities in the background?

It was as if he had visited the rooms of a famous art gallery and, instead of admiring the paintings, had spent his time looking at the floor to see whether it needed repairing.

He lay his head on the desk and quickly took stock of his life.

He had had loving parents that instilled good values and principles in him. After their death, he still felt as if he could communicate with them, especially during those moments of immense uncertainty which life often reserves for people devoted to understanding what goes on in this world, and in some way participating in it.

He had experienced love-passion.

He had survived a horrendous ordeal.

He had become a Jesuit and learned how to work well behind the scenes and get things done, over the opposition of religious and political bureaucracies....

And what did all of that add up to?

And what importance did all these thoughts have?

The only explanation is that this illusion begins to diverge from the reality of life in order to justify your behavior.

But he hadn't yet obtained clarity nor found the reason for his disillusionment.

It was time to get back to reality.

Padre Brian raised his head and leaned against the backrest of the armchair. He looked at the desk strewn with papers and started to search for his appointment book to see what he had to do the next day.

His eyes fell on two postcards and several pictures lying on the corner of the desk. They were from Sara and Albert. The pictures showed them holding hands, smiling at the camera.

"Where are they now?" he wondered.

They looked so far away, yet he imagined them close to him.

It seemed like the days spent with them happened just yesterday, but in fact they had been gone a long time.

A few months after they'd left, Albert had sold all he owned in the Yucatan through an agent—his home and the furniture inside.

At first, he and Sara had kept up contact with Padre Brian by telephone, letters and email. But after six months or so, when they set out on a long journey together, letters and phone calls became occasional postcards.

Now they were far way in the world, like all the people that had left a particular emotional imprint on his life.

Close, yet far away.

He had to admit that the most important experience in his life had been his encounter with love-passion – for many a much-sought-after chimera, difficult to obtain. He had been lucky. Perhaps the briefness of that experience and its dramatic end, which still struck him as unjust, had actually kept the event alive, real and uncontaminated over time.

He found himself smiling because a new thought struck him: Everything was part of the evolution of nature – in the changing of events, in the period of time that is given to us.

He raised his head to the ceiling and said out loud. "Why do you feel so mixed up?

You've done your best as far as love and hope for the future go. You've been able to control your unjustified urges."

He recalled a story the old Jesuit priest used to tell. He could still hear his former teacher's voice and inflections as if it were yesterday.

"A former pupil of mine paid me a visit after many years. Talking about this and that, I inquired as to whether he still attended mass. He said he did not. Then I asked if he were still of the faith, and if he still believed in the afterlife, and in human relationships based on mutual respect, and in pursuing love in the widest meaning of the word.

The man replied with great firmness, 'Those are the principles I've based my existence on, the reasons for which I act, work, communicate. I truly believe in them, and never forget them, in the most important moments and the most insignificant ones of my life, even when I make mistakes'"

Padre Brian remembered how the old Jesuit paused here, before sharing his response to his visitor.

"That is more than enough. I am happy for you and, as your former teacher, derive satisfaction from this."

Padre Brian smiled at the notion "former pupil and former teacher." True learning and teaching, for good or otherwise, was not bound by time.

He was sure of this, whether as a result of divine will or thanks to his own personal experiences in learning and living, or more simply through his own intuition.

Whatever the case, too much time had gone by for Padre Brian to bring the origins of such faith to trial.

It was there, and that was enough.

A shiver ran up his spine, all the way to the nape of his neck. His eyes moistened with joy and he decided the time had come to call it a day.

Tomorrow a full schedule awaited him, but before going to the kindergarten, he would stop at the store and buy some candy to give to the children. And then he would watch them laugh, and share in their laughter, as only the childhood that is in all of us can give us the chance to do.

AFTERWORD

I literally grew up in a motor vehicle factory.

Day after day, from my earliest childhood, I lived amid the production lines of all sorts of two-, three- and four-wheel vehicles. The factory churned out quantities of motorcycles, mini-vans, and later, the famous Isetta—an egg-shaped city vehicle with a front door that opened in such a way as to allow entry without ever having to bend down. We then moved to building sports cars (the various IsoRivolta models), snow mobiles, and a series of Formula 1 racers (the IsoRivolta Marlboro)—just to name a few of our sexiest products.

The factory, our home and the extensive tree-covered grounds were all surrounded by the same wall, and life there was a kind of symbiosis of these three elements. The entire complex occupied most of downtown Bresso, a small town outside Milan, Italy. Inside that little world, successes and problems united people, animals and things.

Two well-defined classes of people gravitated round the facilities. There were those who were part of the factory organization, who either spent their days at the plant or worked beyond the gates to defend the firm's colors in other parts of Italy and abroad; and there were those from the outside world who came to us—customers, visitors and journalists. The former felt as if they belonged to one big family —a feeling that most of them retained even after moving on (myself included). The "outsiders," who often hailed from far and wide, were always thought of as friends of the business and the family and were treated accordingly.

With them, they brought a variety of customs, as well as problems that needed solving, and most of all, a boundless store of enthusiasm which, indeed, proved contagious. You see, at our factory we produced some very special, unique objects that men often fell in love with – perhaps because they had wheels and could be driven; perhaps because they went fast and never talked back.

My father had a magnetic personality and was extremely generous. He died in 1966 at the age of 57, during a slump in the business. I was 25 at the time, a newlywed with a degree in mechanical engineering that I'd received less than a year before from the Polytechnic University of Milan. I had to shift into high gear while still mourning the loss of my dad, whose passing left a scar in me that has never completely vanished.

Luckily, during my university years I had only attended those afternoon application sessions in which attendance was mandatory, while my mornings were spent at the plant. Even as a youngster, my favorite after-school activity had always been hanging round the factory. I still have warm memories of the friendships I made there. Though I never got the highest grades, I breezed through my engineering studies thanks to the rich human and practical experience I had gained inside my father's factory. Upon his passing I took the helm and was caught up by the same frenzy that had marked his life. I burned with the desire to create, to take risks; I had inherited a credo of seeking out new experiences, knowledge, and sensations. Joy came in making new and beautiful things that procured happiness for us as well as for others. Most of all, my father had transmitted to me the longing to always be a free man, to be the master, as far as it is possible, of one's own destiny, able to assume life's responsibilities without being overly influenced by boards of directors, important committees, religions and, especially, political ideologies and politics in general. His lifestyle had shown me that one could ignore geographical and cultural boundaries artificially set up by men, and look at the world with a much broader perspective. This vision of life, which he handed down to me, has led me along paths that at times have been quite difficult, paths where one is sometimes left standing powerless and looking on as positive human power is squandered and lost.

After experiences in different parts of Italy and the world, I literally dropped anchor—I arrived via sailboat—in the beautiful and cultured city of Sarasota, which lies on Florida's west coast, looking out across the Gulf of Mexico. It is here I hope to remain, until one day my ashes are dispersed by the waters of the Gulf.

I still keep that memory of the big yellow villa, my home in the green, wooded estate outside Milan, and of my life in that busy industrial city of northern Italy. My family still owns an apartment on the ground floor of the old villa, with a bit of yard just for ourselves, amid what has become Renzo Rivolta Public Park. I return every so often, when I can manage a break from my hectic schedule, and the place is like a safe, quiet oasis for me, where I am soothed by the house's thick walls, the trees I know one by one because I have watched them grow; many I even planted myself.

The need for open space and freedom inculcated in me by my father, along with his own strange physical need for adrenaline, have driven me to seek out a life brimming with experiences and changes. To begin with, I brushed aside all the rules which people usually adhere to if they want to make a successful career for themselves or simply become rich. The first of these rules is build yourself a resume, a business card that clearly identifies who you are, what you do and how you do it. You work to make this resume more and more credible, until you reach a point where the system itself just drags you along. As long as you don't make any huge blunders, you've passed the test—you don't have to be first in the class any more, or prove that you yourself actually ever attain all that you set out to.

A publisher once asked me to write the story of my life. Who knows whether I'll ever have the time, or even whether it's been interesting enough to entertain readers? For now, I'd be stuck in finding a fil rouge to make the whole thing comprehensible. All I can put on my business card is my name and the name of the company I work for, which are one and the same. There is one single constant in my life, though: the straightforwardness and stubbornness with which I cope with life's daily challenges.

On the work front, I have built sports cars, snowmobiles and Formula 1 racers; I've raised horses in the country and managed a riding stable; I've designed and developed a variety of transport vehicles, including quadricycles, electric cars and buses. I've even organized music festivals, one of which I am particularly proud: La Musica, the International Chamber Music Festival in Sarasota. Over the years, I have constructed factories and directed a large textile mill; I have built office and apartment buildings, shopping centers, marinas and fairly large-sized communities with different amenities, including tennis, golf and horse riding clubs; I have co-founded a bank. My latest madness involved the design and construction of yachts. I'm no longer a young fellow, but I still have plenty of projects in the hopper.

All this surely runs against the grain when it comes to the cultural and economic trends of our times. Today success is measured more in terms of quantity than quality. And it seems that only a precise, repetitive and unrelenting marketing image can succeed in reaching sought-after sales results. This way of thinking doesn't bother me in the slightest, it's just that, unfortunately, I can't apply it—I can't live it. I consider this one of my limitations.

Sometimes I ask myself how I've been able to survive, keep my own company going and progress. I think that while quantity may mean business, passion and quality are protected by the spirit that makes the world go round. I look out and gaze upon the city lights in the distance and listen to the far-off hum, entranced, indulging myself in the awareness of being a poet, in the same sense that we can all be poets.

I felt these reflections on my own life were important because *The Castaway* is but a simple story written by a man who sees, thinks and acts with great simplicity and believes that such simplicity is part of the world's true poetry. I don't mean only written poetry, but those magical moments in which thought, nature, rationality, efficiency, human relationships, battles, tragedies, victories, conquests, gains, losses, illnesses, quarrels, and good times remind us that it's all just a game we can always get out of—not always unscathed, but in any case, we do get out. We just have to open our eyes and try to understand that behind any complicated situation lies a simple explanation. Perhaps too simple to be grasped, since for centuries we've been taught to reason according to very complex schemes. It is only by complicating simple things that people with no particular talent succeed in controlling the world. Let's take a minute out and think it over. We may get lucky. Lightning may strike and ignite, within our minds, a flash of poetry, of creation.

Piero Rivolta, Sarasota 2010

ACKNOWLEDGMENTS

It is very important for me to acknowledge all the people who have been so patient to put up with me in the process of transforming my manuscript into a real book. Unfortunately, the only way I know how to interpret my thoughts is to put them down on paper with a fountain pen; I am very meticulous in what I write, but my handwriting is horrible.

A special thank-you goes to John Rugman, an American who has chosen to live in Turin, Italy, for his translation of my book into English. Vanessa Houston has been patient and judicious in her support. Chris Angermann has helped with editing and shepherding this book to the printer. And last, but not least, thanks to my dear long-time friend Richard Storm, who continues to take care of my public relationship, even though he is semi-retired. He has contributed his sage advice at various milestones along this journey.